THE KINDERGARTEN CAPER

Roy MacGregor

D0059585

McClelland & Stewart

To Douglas Gibson, who years ago had this crazy idea
for kids' hockey books

Library and Archives Canada Cataloguing in Publication

MacGregor, Roy, 1948–
    The kindergarten caper : the Screech Owls prequel / Roy MacGregor.

ISBN 978-0-7710-5608-6

    I. Title.

PS8575.G84K55 2008   jC813'.54   C2008-901204-6

We acknowledge the financial support of the Government of Canada through the Book Publishing Industry Development Program and that of the Government of Ontario through the Ontario Media Development Corporation's Ontario Book Initiative. We further acknowledge the support of the Canada Council for the Arts and the Ontario Arts Council for our publishing program.

Typeset in Bembo by M&S, Toronto
Printed and bound in Canada

McClelland & Stewart Ltd.
75 Sherbourne Street
Toronto, Ontario
M5A 2P9
www.mcclelland.com

1 2 3 4 5   12 11 10 09 08

TRAVIS LINDSAY LOOKED OVER AT SARAH Cuthbertson, and both of them, at exactly the same time, rolled their eyes toward the ceiling.

How many times – in all the years they had been in the same grade and on the same hockey team – had they shared this same look? And how many times had it involved Wayne Nishikawa – *Nish* – the Screech Owls' best defenceman and Travis's best friend in the world, not to mention the most self-centred, most attention-seeking, most self-glorifying twelve-year-old that had ever lived?

The Screech Owls had been invited to take the magnificent trophy they had won at the Bell Capital Cup in Ottawa and show it off to the lower grades at Lord Stanley Public School. They had started the day in Miss Robinson's kindergarten class. And as he talked to the five-year-olds sitting in their tiny chairs, Nish, as always, was holding court. The little kids' eyes were big as saucers as Nish explained how he, too, had once sat in this very same kindergarten classroom (before he became one of the greatest stars of the hockey world), and how he had once rescued the little screech owl called Stanley who had inspired the name of the town's most famous hockey team.

Sarah eased over and whispered in Travis's ear. "Wouldn't they just love to hear the *real* story . . ."

Travis giggled. Would they ever!

As Nish's story got more and more unbelievable, Travis couldn't help but think back to the day they had entered this same classroom for the very first time . . .

2

"*AAAAAEEEEEEEEEEYYYYYYYYYY!!!!!!*"

Never in Travis Lindsay's so-far-unremarkable five years of life on this earth had he heard such a scream.

Not when his grandmother's cat took a cuff at his face and stuck a claw half-way up his bloodied nostril.

Not when his father accidentally slammed his own hand in the car door (though Travis did learn several new words he had never heard before).

Not even when Travis had woken up a week ago from the worst nightmare of his little life – screaming hysterically at the green-faced witches and winged monkeys that had chased him all through the night after his parents rented some movie about a little girl named Dorothy and her dog, Toto, who were carried away by a tornado. Mr. and Mrs. Lindsay thought Travis would enjoy seeing what they said was their favourite movie. Now he desperately hoped they never rented one they *didn't* like.

But, no, none of those screams was even remotely like this.

"*AAAAAEEEEEEEEEEEYYYYYYYYYYYY!!!!!!*"

There it was again.

Travis knew where it was coming from. That was obvious. Miss Robinson — the curly-haired lady in glasses at the front of the class — had welcomed them all to their very first day of kindergarten by marching them around the big basement classroom and showing them everything they would need to know.

She showed them the cloakroom, where they could hang their jackets and, in winter, get into and out of their big coats and winter boots and toques and mittens.

She showed them the blackboard and the chalk and how to clean the boards. She showed them where the paper was for art and where she kept the jars filled with crayons and pencils and watercolour pens.

She showed them the small library of pop-up books and picture books and even a few books with words in them, prompting one tiny little kid with thick glasses — Travis thought his name was Simon — to volunteer that he was already reading "at a Grade-Two level." Travis disliked him instantly.

She showed them what she called her "nature club" — an area with posters of lakes and trees and wildlife all along one wall. The "club" was set off from the rest of the room by a fence made from tree

4

branches, some with dried leaves still clinging to them. Behind the branches were several aquariums, a number of small cages, and shelves of fascinating things like porcupine quills, abandoned bird nests, turtle shells, and unusual rocks. Travis was already mad crazy to join Miss Robinson's nature club.

But then, lastly, she had showed them what seemed her true pride and joy. The toilet.

Over the summer, the school had built a new washroom right inside the kindergarten classroom. It had its own walls, of course, and a door, but the walls didn't quite go all the way to the ceiling. Miss Robinson liked it because the kids no longer needed a teacher or one of the bigger students from next door to walk them all the way down the long hallway to the big "students" washroom. Travis had already been in there in the spring, when his mother brought him to the school to register him for the fall. It was *huge*, with almost no privacy. Travis figured it would take an enormous burst of courage – roughly similar to taking on the Wicked Witch of the North – merely to go about one's business in such a public place.

Miss Robinson was clearly delighted with her new addition – *relieved* might be a better word – and she explained the process: "If you need to go, put up your hand and wait for me to nod that it's okay."

Everyone had wondered who would be first to raise a hand.

How mortifying, Travis thought. You might as well put up a flashing sign telling everyone you were about to go into that little cubicle and make the most embarrassing noises imaginable.

Travis couldn't stand the idea of anyone hearing him go. He could only imagine what that cute little girl with the blond ponytail – *Sarah?* – would think if she heard him splashing around in there.

He could, of course, if he was very careful, arrange to make no sound at all – but no sound would be even *worse*! The last thing Travis Lindsay, future superstar in the National Hockey League, needed was for the entire class to know that he, a man (well, at least a small boy), *sat down to pee*!

Travis had decided, at that very moment, he would never, ever, use the new kindergarten washroom. No matter what. No matter even if he burst like one of those water balloons the bigger boys on his street sometimes dropped off garage roofs to see them explode on the driveway.

So, who would be first?

Miss Robinson continued telling them how the school worked, and what all those bells meant, and how the kindergarten would have recess in a fenced-in area of the schoolyard away from the bigger kids . . . when, suddenly, a hand went up. A hand that shook slightly as it slowly rose.

Travis wasn't surprised. It was the fat kid with

the super-red face – almost as if he had come to school already embarrassed. What was the kid's name? Wayne something? And a last name no one would ever be able to remember. *Nincompoop?* Travis giggled to himself at his little joke. Yes, *Nincompoop!* He would have to call the chubby red-faced kid that. He'd have to make sure everyone called him that.

Travis had been dropped off early by his dad, as the school was on Mr. Lindsay's route to work. It had been simple enough. His father had pulled up to the curb, reached back, and opened the rear door. Travis had unbuckled himself and stepped out with his little backpack. Mr. Lindsay had winked and wished Travis luck. The door had shut and away sped the car.

Not so with little Mr. Nincompoop. The stupid red-faced kid had waddled up to the kindergarten entrance with his mother in tow, the two of them sobbing like babies. His mother knelt down and wrapped her arms around the snotty little kid and carried on as if she'd never see him again.

She should be so lucky, thought Travis.

The chubby kid had sniffled constantly after his mother left him. He'd blown his nose into his shirt as they stood in line, and he'd whimpered like a little puppy while Miss Robinson checked off their names and assigned each child a seat. Travis was happy the kid with the tomato face would be sitting nowhere near him.

And then, just before what would be the first recess of Travis Lindsay's short life, the Nincompoop had put up his hand to go to the toilet.

Miss Robinson nodded, and the red-faced boy got up, waddled across the room to the washroom, and disappeared inside. Every kid in the room watched him go . . . and then listened for him to *go*.

There were giggles as the expected tinkling sound reached them over the washroom walls. "Shush, now!" Miss Robinson said sternly, raising a finger to her lips.

And then came a completely unexpected sound: "*AAAAAEEEEEEEEEEYYYYYYYYYYYY!!!!!!*"

Miss Robinson hurried over to the door and rapped twice hard. "Wayne? You alright in there?"

"*I'M STUCK!*" the Nincompoop bawled.

Miss Robinson looked bewildered. *Stuck?* Stuck in the toilet seat? No – otherwise, there wouldn't have been all that tinkling. Was the door stuck?

"*I'M STUCK, IN MY ZIPPER!*" the Nincompoop wailed.

The realization washed over Miss Robinson's face as if someone had coloured her in with one of the red crayons. She was as beet-red as the chubby little kid who was first to try out the new toilet.

Travis looked across the way at the little girl with

the ponytail. Sarah was laughing out loud and trying to hide her face on her desk.

Travis didn't dare laugh out loud. The last thing he wanted was to get in trouble with Miss Robinson. But inside, he was howling, he was slapping his knees, he was holding his gut. Inside, he was choking he was laughing so hard at the stupid Nincompoop.

"Stay where you are!" Miss Robinson called through the door. "I'll get help!" She seemed in a state of panic. She pushed the intercom button, and a woman in the office, speaking in a very calm voice, came on the speaker. Miss Robinson, sputtering, was suddenly unable to say anything at all. The woman in the office had to ask a second time before Miss Robinson was finally able to say something. "Send the janitor down here, *quick*!" she said, near shouting. ". . . And have him bring his tools!"

The office signed off. Miss Robinson went back to the washroom door and spoke into it as if it, too, were an intercom system. "Just stay where you are! Help is on the way!"

"*I'm stuck!*" the Nincompoop whined through his bawling. "*I think I'm bleeding!*"

Miss Robinson checked the clock, wringing her hands. It was almost recess.

There was a knock at the classroom door, and a man came in carrying a tool box. It was the janitor, a tall, thin man, wearing coveralls with an identification tag pinned over the chest. He was almost completely bald, but his gigantic moustache was hairy enough to cover his entire head if he'd wanted.

"I have a boy, *stuck*, in the washroom, Mr. Greeley," Miss Robinson said.

"You want me to pull him out?" the janitor asked.

"Not that kind of stuck," she said, reddening. "*Stuck* . . . stuck in his zipper . . . you know . . ."

Mr. Greeley considered a moment, twirling his moustache, and then made a smile so big it seemed the ends of the moustache were going to reach up and high-five each other.

"Ahhh," said the janitor. "Sounds like a job for pliers. And maybe work gloves, too." He winked at Miss Robinson, who blushed even deeper.

Travis looked across at Sarah again. She was holding her stomach.

Mr. Greeley opened his tool box, took out pliers and work gloves, put on the gloves, and knocked at the door.

"Okay if I come in?" he asked.

A small voice whimpered from within: "*Y-yes . . .*"

Mr. Greeley winked again and opened the door and stepped inside. No one said a word. Everyone was waiting to hear what would happen. It seemed no one was even breathing.

There was a snipping sound and a loud click, then the sound of a zipper being opened and closed again.

"Good as new, boy," the janitor's voice came from inside the washroom. "Good as new."

The door opened, and the janitor came out, followed by the Nincompoop. His shirt was wet with tears. His eyes were so red, it looked like someone had shaken salt into them. His fat red face was swollen as if it had been boiled in a big pot.

"Okay now, Wayne?" Miss Robinson asked.

The Nincompoop started to cry again.

Travis Lindsay looked over at Sarah and both shook their heads in bewilderment.

What a loser . . .

3

TRAVIS KNEW HIS MOTHER WAS TALKING TO THE mother of someone else in the kindergarten class. She had been on the telephone a couple of times already this evening, and though Travis never once heard the words "stuck" or "zipper," he knew from his mom's throaty giggles that she was being filled in on the Great Kindergarten Toilet Crisis.

Finally, the calls were over. She hung up the telephone and came into the living room, were Travis and his father were watching the early sports highlights. "That was Mrs. Cuthbertson," Mrs. Lindsay said to them. "Sarah's mother."

Sarah? The girl in the ponytail?

"She seems really nice," Mrs. Lindsay continued. "They've just moved in a couple of streets over, and she was hoping you and Sarah could walk to school together in the morning. Fine with you, Trav?"

Travis tried to make it sound as if he couldn't care one way or the other. "I guess," he said.

"And Mrs. Cuthbertson has been talking to another neighbour, a Mrs. . . . Oh, darn, I forget just now. Anyway, she's a single parent and can't walk her boy to class each morning, so Sarah's mom suggested the three of you walk together."

"I guess," Travis said again, though with distinctly less enthusiasm.

"The new boy's name is Wayne," Mrs. Cuthbertson added, before heading back into the kitchen.

Travis's heart suddenly sank.

No . . . Please . . . Not the Nincompoop!

• • •

It was raining in the morning – hard, driving drops that seemed to bounce off the back deck like machine-gun fire as Travis, wearing his Pittsburgh Penguins pyjamas, stood by the glass doors and contemplated what would be his second day of school.

A day already ruined by having to walk to school with the Nincompoop.

He hoped the rain would fall even harder – that way, he'd be driven to school by his father. Perhaps Sarah could come with them . . . but *not* the Nincompoop.

Travis comforted himself with this thought over a breakfast of Froot Loops and banana slices. But it wasn't to be. His father came down dressed for work, leaned tight to the window over the sink, and noted that the rain seemed to be letting up. The radio was also calling for clearing, and just as his father headed out for the day the telephone rang. It was Sarah's mother, calling to say Sarah was ready.

"I'll see you to the corner," Travis's mother said to him.

The rain had stopped and was already steaming off the road and sidewalk as they set out. Travis had his Pittsburgh Penguins backpack on and his Pittsburgh Penguins cap. He wondered if anyone else in Miss Robinson's kindergarten class was as hockey mad as he was.

"There they are!" Mrs. Lindsay called, waving down the street to a tall woman who looked like a grown-up version of the girl standing beside her. Both were blond, both had ponytails, both were wearing blue jeans and red tops, but only one, the smaller one, had a backpack. Take away the backpack, Travis thought, and they'd be like the set of Russian dolls his grandmother kept on the mantle, one large one opening up to produce a series of smaller and smaller ones, all identical. Sarah and her mother looked like the largest doll and the smallest standing beside each other.

The mothers made their introductions and then introduced their kids to each other, though Travis had technically met Sarah already, when Miss Robinson had them introduce themselves to each other.

"Hi, Travis," Sarah said with a big, welcoming smile.

"Hi," Travis said back. He could feel his face burning.

"Off you go, then," Mrs. Cuthbertson said. "You know where the crosswalk is – and make sure you wait to be taken across. Okay?"

"Okay, Mom," said Sarah, who accepted her mother's kiss and immediately headed down the street. Travis took his kiss on the run, hurrying to catch up to the little girl in the ponytail.

"Don't forget," Travis's mom called after them, "you're picking up Wayne at the corner of Lorne and Centre!"

Travis nodded back, then turned and ran a few steps more to catch up to Sarah.

"Can't we go another way and avoid this kid?" Travis suggested.

Sarah laughed. "I wouldn't miss this for the world," she said. "He's like having a home entertainment centre right in the classroom."

"You *like* him?"

"I didn't say I *liked* him – I said I find him entertaining. You weren't bored yesterday, were you?"

"No, but . . ."

"Well, what do you remember most about yesterday – where Miss Robinson keeps the art paper or the kid getting stuck in his own zipper?"

"I don't know. The kid, I guess, but that doesn't mean we have to like him!"

"No, but it does mean we have to watch him. He's different."

Travis couldn't argue with that.

"There they are!" Sarah announced.

Up ahead, waiting on the corner, was the Nincompoop. He was holding his mother's hand as if he were a toddler in a shopping mall. Travis loved his mother, but he didn't like it much anymore when she tried holding his hand – particularly when other kids were around. After all, he was *five years old*. But this kid looked like he *had* to have hold of his mother's hand. Otherwise, it seemed to Travis, he might just collapse into a lump of quivering jelly and be washed into the nearest storm sewer and away.

If only, thought Travis.

In her other hand, the Nincompoop's mother was holding an umbrella – the rain had begun to fall lightly again – and the two were squeezed in under it. Travis couldn't help but note that mother and son had roughly the same shape: round. He wondered what the father looked like. Apart from their shape, mother and son sure didn't look the same: she was fair-skinned and with light brown hair; he was dark-haired and red-faced.

"Hello, children," the woman said. She had a nice smile, Travis noticed, even though he hated being referred to as a child. "Wayne's been telling me all about you two."

Huh? What could this chubby little guy possibly know about them? Travis looked at Sarah, and she rolled her eyes. She obviously felt the same. He looked at Wayne, who was acting so angelic for his mother it was a wonder he wasn't wearing a halo and wings.

What . . . a . . . loser! Travis thought to himself.

The Nincompoop's mother knelt and gave her son a big wet kiss on the cheek, and he kissed her back and they hugged.

Travis cringed. Had he no shame? He noticed tears in the mother's eyes – or was it just rain? – and wondered how a simple morning goodbye could seem like the world was coming to an end.

Another quick peck on her boy's cheek, and Wayne's mother stood back up, smiling sadly. It was tears, Travis decided. Not rain. Real tears.

The three little kindergarten students walked on, Wayne turning periodically to wave back to his mother, who stood still under her umbrella, as sad a sight as Travis could imagine.

"What's your last name again?" Sarah asked.

"Nishikawa," Wayne answered.

"What's *that*?" Travis asked.

"Japanese," the chubby little kid answered. "My father's dead. I'm all my mom has now – which makes me special."

17

Travis winced. What a way to talk about yourself.

"You can call me Nish," Wayne said. "That's what they called my dad when he was alive. 'Nish' is good."

Nish? Travis thought. What kind of a name was that?

TRAVIS LOOKED DOWN THE STREET TOWARD THE school. The maples were still in their summer glory, their high branches forming a ragged green canopy for as far as he could see. He suddenly felt very small. And unsure. He had never walked this far before on his own.

"C'mon!" Sarah said, her voice full of enthusiasm and confidence. She stepped lightly ahead, as if she were skipping down the Yellow Brick Road. The Nincompoop . . . Wayne . . . *Nish* . . . on the other hand, moved like he was climbing a mountain and had run short of oxygen. He was dragging his new backpack by the strap along the sidewalk. Travis wondered how it was going to survive even a week of school.

"My mom says you're signing up for hockey," Sarah said to Travis.

"Yeah," Travis answered, suddenly reddening with importance.

"I'm signing up, too," Sarah said.

"*Girls* don't play hockey," a voice whined from behind. It was the Nincompoop. Travis couldn't believe the way he said "girls." It sounded like his grandmother when she found signs of mice at the cottage. Or like his grandfather when he stepped in some dog droppings at the park that day.

"*Girls* play with dolls," the whining continued. "*Girls* play piano. *Girls* play hide-and-seek. *Girls* play skipping. *Girls* play nurse. *Girls* play ringette."

Sarah cut him off. "I play ringette, too. And the piano. And with dolls. What exactly do you do, Mr. Smartypants?"

"I moon people," said the chubby kid.

Sarah turned on her heels to face him. "*You what?*"

The Nincompoop was grinning, his face like a carved pumpkin that was slightly off-colour. "I moon people."

"You're *sick*," Sarah said, shaking her head and picking up the pace as she hurried ahead of the grinning kid.

Travis was baffled. "What do you mean, you 'moon' people?" he asked.

"You don't know what mooning is?" the new kid giggled.

"Don't ask," Sarah snapped back. "You don't want to know!"

But Travis did want to know. He turned to walk backwards, waiting for the Nincompoop to answer.

"I'll show you," the new kid said, his grin even wider now. In an instant, he tossed his backpack onto the grass, turned around, undid his belt.

Travis went into shock! He looked down the street. A yellow school bus was coming, and behind it a string of impatient traffic waiting for the bus to turn in at the school.

Down went the pants to the ankles. Down went the underwear.

"*What're you doing?*" Travis screamed.

But the new kid was laughing from his crouched position. He wiggled his bare bottom at Travis. "This, my friend, is mooning!"

Travis felt his face burning. His heart was in his mouth. He could feel sweat popping out on his forehead.

What if the school-bus driver saw? What if there was a police car behind the bus? What if they got . . . *caught*? Travis's imagination was spinning. He saw the three of them in the back of a police car. He saw himself phoning home and having to tell his mother that he hadn't made it to kindergarten, that instead he was in jail. He saw his father coming to get him, Mr. Lindsay with that look on his face that Travis had long ago learned to avoid if at all possible. He saw himself walking out – in handcuffs and leg irons, with two gigantic police officers pushing him forward – to face his father and try to explain the completely unexplainable.

Travis shuddered.

The rain was just a sprinkle now, cool on his burning face as he hurried to catch up to Sarah. She had moved considerably ahead.

As he caught up to Sarah, Travis spun back for one more look. The Nincompoop was laughing, his big shoulders shaking, as he buckled his pants back up and leaned over to scoop up his backpack.

Travis was out of breath. It wasn't from running; he was out of breath for another reason. *Fear?*

He felt terrible for Sarah. A girl shouldn't have to see such things. How could that Nincompoop do such a thing in front of her?

He turned to apologize to her. He didn't know what reaction he had expected. Maybe he thought she'd be angry, or in tears. Maybe she'd be pretending it hadn't happened. But not this. She was *laughing*. Sarah was laughing as she walked. She had a smile as wide as the janitor's moustache. She might even have been crying, she was laughing so hard, though it was impossible to tell with the way the rain was spotting her cheeks.

"I told you he was interesting," she said.

Travis was dumbfounded. He had no idea what to say.

"I think kindergarten is going to be fun," she said. "A *lot* of fun."

WHAT WAS *WITH* THAT KID?

Travis had never met anyone quite like the Nincompoop – okay, "Nish," or whatever stupid name he wanted to be called by – and he found himself going through the strangest experience because of this new kid with the fat red face. He couldn't stand him, but he couldn't stop watching him.

It was the second day of kindergarten and Nish was already the talk of the school. Several big Grade Fours had been on the school bus that Nish had mooned, and at morning recess they'd come over to the fenced-off area where the kindergarten kids played and started pointing at Nish.

Only they hadn't come to tell on him, but to treat him like he was some sort of hero. And Nish, to make matters worse, was soaking it up like he was a television star meeting his fans. Travis couldn't believe it. Nish was laughing and talking to the

Grade Fours like he was in Grade Five or Six himself, not a lowly kindergartener who shouldn't even expect a Grade Four to give him a second thought.

Nish seemed in his glory. Travis edged over close enough to pick up part of the conversation. What he heard the chubby little kid telling the Grade Fours stunned him.

"This is actually my second kindergarten," Nish was telling them. "I got kicked out of school last year."

"What for?" one of the boys asked over the fence.

"Smoking," Nish answered.

"*Smoking?*" several surprised Grade Fours said at once.

Nish nodded knowingly, as if it were the simplest statement imaginable. "Yeah . . ." he said, pausing dramatically, "cigars."

The eyes of the Grade Fours opened so wide it was a wonder their eyeballs didn't roll out. "*No way!*" one shouted.

"Way," Nish said, and pretended to flick an ash from the end of his finger.

Travis looked across to the other side of the group, where Sarah was huddled with another girl – Jenny, Travis thought her name was. They were giggling as they listened in.

He realized now that all the kindergarten kids were gathered there by the fence. The smart kid called Simon with his smudged glasses. The tiny little kid called Jeremy, who had come to school with a goalie mini-stick in his backpack. The dark, skinny little kid with the name that rhymed with "odd" – was it Fahd? The kid who'd told Miss Robinson he could fix the class computer if it ever broke down (Travis thought Miss Robinson had called him Larry or something, but this Fahd, who seemed to be his friend, called him Data, like the guy from the *Star Trek* movies). There were others. A kid called Jesse and one called Wilson. Another one called Willie. A Liz and a Derek. A Gordie. And one with a very odd name – Dmitri? Tall kids, short kids, shy kids . . . but only one Nish, thank heavens.

All the kindergarten kids, like all the towering Grade Fours, were listening to this chubby little kid with the red face like he was some rock star – the very same kid who'd bawled when his mother had dropped him off, who had caught himself in his zipper, who had mooned the school bus.

It made no sense. They should have been howling with laughter at him for what he'd done in the washroom. They should have been shaking their head in disgust over how he'd behaved when his mother dropped him off for the first day of class. They should have been turning him over to the police for what he'd done on the street that morning to the school bus.

But no – they were treating him like a hero. And worse, he was acting as if it were exactly the way he deserved to be treated.

Travis felt he no longer knew right from wrong, up from down. It was as if everything he had ever been taught or thought he knew about life had suddenly been marked "WRONG" by the teacher.

Nish was still talking. "It was a real tough school, yeah – we had kids in Grade Six coming on motorcycles. We had to go through metal detectors in every classroom. They had armed guards escorting the teachers from room to room. Tough town. Nothing like this place at all."

Travis felt a tug at his sleeve. It was Sarah, pulling him away. She had tears running down her cheeks. She was laughing so hard she could hardly catch her breath.

"He's lying," Travis said as they moved away from the gathering by the fence.

"Of course he is," Sarah said. "But it's funny."

"Lying's not funny," Travis said. "It's wrong. You get in trouble."

"Something tells me our new friend is going to get in a lot of trouble."

"What do you mean, 'new friend'?" Travis snapped. "He's no *friend*. He's a weirdo."

Sarah stopped and shrugged. "I kind of like him," she said with a smile. "He makes things interesting."

It was getting louder by the fence. One of the bigger kids was shouting. "What's this we hear about one of you little kinder-babies getting stuck in his own fly?" The other kids were laughing. The story must have been all over the school by now. Perhaps the janitor had told.

"Who *was* it?" one of the Grade Four girls screamed at Nish, who was now the colour of an over-ripe tomato.

"Who?"

"Yeah, *who*?"

"You want to know *who*?"

Nish was laughing *with* the big kids. He stepped back from the fence, turned, and pointed. *Right at Travis!*

"That's the guy," Nish said, shaking his head in mock disgust. "That's Zipper Boy."

TRAVIS THOUGHT HE WAS STILL DREAMING.

His father was sitting on the edge of his bed, gently grasping Travis's shoulder and giving him periodic shakes. Travis could feel himself drifting in and out of the moment, almost as if he were drowning and couldn't help going back down again – except down into deep sleep, not deep water.

"Time to get up, son," Mr. Lindsay was saying. "We're on the ice in an hour."

Travis shook his head, pulled free of the sleep that was tugging him back down. *Ice?* Yes, today was Saturday! No school! Today was the first day of hockey practice! The first practice *ever*!

It seemed to Travis that he had been waiting for this moment almost all his life. That wasn't much of an exaggeration, either. When he was two, his father had built their first backyard rink, and for the last two winters he had been skating without the help of chairs or grown-ups' hands and was even getting pretty good with a hockey stick and puck.

He was headed for the National Hockey League. He would be following a family tradition. His father's distant cousin – actually, his grandfather's cousin – was Ted Lindsay, member of the Hockey Hall of Fame and legendary teammate of Gordie Howe. It had been Ted Lindsay, as captain of the Detroit Red Wings, who had been the first NHL player ever to raise the Stanley Cup over his head and then skate around the rink with it. How Travis Lindsay wished to do that himself one day . . .

Ted Lindsay had been a formidable player. He had played in more than a thousand NHL games between 1944 and 1965. He had once retired for four years and then came back and played as if he'd merely sat out a shift. He scored more than a thousand points, averaging more than a point a game in the playoffs. He won four Stanley Cups, the scoring championship, and was elected to the Hockey Hall of Fame.

And, like Travis, he had been a little guy – small for his age even when he was all grown up. But he was tough. So tough, in fact, that his NHL nickname had been Terrible Ted.

Travis had desperately wanted his own nickname for some time now. He thought he was too polite to ever be known as Terrible Travis, but he hoped to be a good-enough hockey player to be known one day as Terrific Travis or Two-Goal Travis.

Not *Zipper Boy*! Yet that was exactly the nick-name he'd been stuck with for the past three days of school, the bigger kids in the schoolyard yelling it out at recess and even hanging halfway out the school-bus windows to scream it as they passed the three little kindergarten students making their way along the street.

Sarah, Nish . . . and Zipper Boy.

Travis had never hated anyone so much in his short life as he hated this Nish Nincompoop.

"Up and at 'em," his father said. "Your breakfast is on the table. I'll check your equipment bag. We'll be picking up Sarah on the way."

Travis had forgotten that the little girl with the ponytail had signed up for hockey, too. Sarah would see how well Travis could skate. She'd be impressed. He'd be a star in her eyes.

And he'd no longer be Zipper Boy.

7

TRAVIS WISHED HE WERE BACK IN THE kindergarten classroom – but only so the toilet would be close by. He couldn't stop dancing. He'd already gone to the bathroom twice, his father kidding him about "drinking too much," and now he had to go again.

Too excited. Too wound up.

His father was helping him put on his equipment. It was the first time Travis had ever officially dressed for hockey, but likely the hundredth time he had put on the little shin pads, shoulder pads, elbow pads, neck guard, helmet, gloves, skates, and, of course, jock.

He had his stick – measured and cut by his father so it came to just under his chin when he was on skates – and his father had helped him tape it. "Always use black tape, Trav," Mr. Lindsay had said. "Makes it more difficult for the goalies to pick up your shot. Use white tape and they can see the puck all the way."

His father had tightened Travis's skates and run some shin-pad tape around the outside of his socks. Then he'd helped him with the jersey he'd been assigned for the practice. Travis didn't care for the number, 19, and his father told him the name printed across the back had something to do with the Tamarack hardware store. So it wasn't Terrible Ted's famous number 7, and it wasn't the colours of the Pittsburgh Penguins or even the Detroit Red Wings – but it was still a real hockey sweater, and it was his.

His father pulled the sweater over Travis's head. Travis felt as if he were entering a room he had never been inside before. The jersey smelled brand new and freshly washed. It felt cool and warm at the same time. He opened his eyes and watched it glide past him as his father pulled it down. As the hardware store crest passed his mouth he kissed the back of it for good luck.

He giggled. What a stupid thing to do. But it still felt right. One day, he hoped, he'd wear an "A" or a "C" on his jersey, for "Assistant Captain" or "Captain" of a team. And if he ever reached that mark, he'd always kiss the back of the magic letter for luck.

Travis was still giggling as his head popped back out through the neck. His father was already fixing the helmet, the cage front lifted high as Mr. Lindsay carefully placed it over Travis's head. He fitted it snugly, then lowered the cage and snapped everything in tight.

Then gloves and stick, and Travis Lindsay, future NHL number 1 draft pick, was ready to go.

He looked around. There were more than a dozen other kids also being readied by parents and older brothers and sisters. He recognized most of them from his kindergarten class – the kid named Jesse, the little know-it-all called Simon, big Gordie, Derek, Wilson, and others – but Sarah was nowhere to be seen.

"Let's get out there," Mr. Lindsay said. He was putting on his own skates. He would be helping as assistant coach, but, as he said to Travis, "Don't laugh, I haven't been on skates since before you were born."

Still, Travis was glad to have his dad there. His father had taught him the game in the driveway and on the school rink, but he'd always worn winter boots rather than skates. His father must have known what he was doing, though, for Travis figured he was already, at least for his age, a pretty good skater.

The Lindsays were first out onto the ice. The Zamboni had just headed off, and one of the rink attendants was scraping the snow away from where the big machine had driven out. That done, he swung the big doors shut and waved for Mr. Lindsay and Travis to start.

Travis loved the way the new ice glistened. It looked as if it had been created just this moment for him to skate on. It was white as wet Ivory soap except where the lines were. He stepped out and breathed in the cold, distinctive air of the arena, filled his lungs and looked around him. He was *first on* — as good a feeling as it gets for a young hockey player. It was as if this ice had never been touched by a skate blade before, even though bigger kids had just left the ice after their practice.

Travis started out, his little legs stuttering as he sought to dig his blades in so he could drive off and away. He had his stick for balance, which helped.

Straight down the ice he went, determined to be first around. He could hear his blades on the ice, but he wasn't big enough, yet, to make that sizzling sound he so loved when the bigger kids took to the ice. The time would come, he knew, when every flick of his ankle would produce that wonderful sound, when ice would spray in a thin arc behind him as he dug in, and every stride would leave its own mark as he headed down the rink and carved hard into his first turn behind the net.

But for now, he was just in beginners. He was probably one of the few kids who could even skate on his own.

He looked to the side as something large passed him. It was his father. Mr. Lindsay was a bit shaky on his skates, but it was obvious he had once been a fine skater. Ice flicked as he dug in. His stride down the ice left a series of lines that curled at each end as he pushed off. It was beautiful to see. Travis could hardly wait to make marks like that on the ice.

The other kids were coming out now, and Travis's heart filled with pride as he realized none of them was up to his level of skating. Some stood. Some skittered forward and fell. Some fell instantly backward. Some held on to the boards. Some had older brothers or sisters, or their mothers or fathers, out to hold them up. It was almost as if they were learning to walk all over again.

Travis could go on his own. He could make turns in both directions and even sprayed a little ice if he reached full speed before turning suddenly to stop. He had never felt so proud in all his life. So much for Zipper Boy – he was now *Skater* Boy!

But then, as he made a rather good turn and began coming up toward the entrance gate again, he saw Sarah. He knew her instantly, the familiar ponytail sticking out the back of her helmet. She came out alone, her father accompanying her only as far as the boards, then standing there, smiling, as Sarah stepped out, jumped a couple of times on her skates as if shaking off cobwebs, and took off down the ice as if she'd been born with skates on.

Travis came to a complete stop and just watched.

Sarah had a perfect style. Instead of taking short, choppy steps like Travis, she used long, graceful strides. She skated as well as anyone else on the ice – parents and coaches included – and she did it without seeming to put even the slightest effort into it.

Travis couldn't believe what he was seeing. The best hockey player on the ice was . . . a . . . *girl*.

There were still more kids to come. Some must have slept in or arrived late. After Sarah came two kids dressed in goalie equipment – Travis thought one was Jeremy from kindergarten, and the other might be Sarah's friend Jennie. Then came the kid with the strange name – *Dmitri?* – who took off like he'd been shot from a cannon, racing around the rink faster than any of the other kids, Sarah included, but without her smooth stride.

Soon they were all out, and the once-fresh ice was scratched all over with skate marks.

A heavy man with a black moustache and a ball cap blew a whistle and called them all to centre ice. As he waited for them to gather, he lifted his cap to scratch his head, revealing a big bald spot.

Travis and Sarah were first over. She leaned over and tapped his shin pads with her stick. "Great to see you, Trav," Sarah said. "You're *good*!" Travis just smiled. He wasn't sure he could speak.

The man with the whistle looked like he could use some coaching himself. He was shaky on his skates, seemed on the verge of flipping upside down as he steadied himself and began checking names off on a clipboard.

He paused, looked up, and winked at the assembled players. "My name's Dillinger," he said. "I'm going to be your first-year coach. I've never coached before, but you've never played before, so we're going to be a good fit. I'm Derek's dad."

Travis looked over at Derek and saw that he was swelling with pride. Travis wished his own father had signed up for coach and not assistant. He could see that his father was a far better skater than Mr. Dillinger. But Mr. Dillinger did seem nice, and Travis instantly took a liking to him.

The coach was going through the names. "Sarah, good to see you. . . . Simon Milliken? Yes, good. . . . Dmitri Yakushev – I see you're already way ahead of the rest of us. Travis Lindsay? Yes, got ya. . . ." As Mr. Dillinger checked off each name, he took note of the kid it belonged to. He seemed to know about half of them already, which was good.

The coach paused at a final name scribbled on his clipboard. He looked about, one eyebrow raised higher than the other. "Wayne . . . Nishi-kiwi?" he asked.

"Nishi*kawa*," Sarah corrected him. "He's not here."

Nish? Travis thought. *Oh, no! Not him!*

"He's just here now," said Derek, pointing toward the entrance.

The entire beginners group turned to look.

Nish and his mother were at the open gate. He was in full hockey gear and hanging on for his life. His face beamed like a brake light through the cage. Mrs. Nishikawa was almost as red, frantically trying to get her chubby little player to stay on his feet, but every time Nish set out, down he went.

"I'll get him," Mr. Lindsay announced.

"Thanks," said Mr. Dillinger.

Mr. Lindsay skated quickly over and picked Nish up off the ice like he was some enormous rag doll. Nish made no effort to help. He just let Mr. Lindsay do all the work.

Travis felt a tap on this shin pads. It was Sarah. "This is going to be fun," she said.

Mr. Lindsay was trying to get Nish to skate by holding him up under the arms, but it was hopeless. Nish just flopped about, and every time Mr. Lindsay let him go, he went down in a heap.

Finally, Mr. Lindsay left him there and skated over to the penalty box. He opened the door, reached in, and pulled out a stacking chair. He carried the chair across the ice to where Nish lay as if he'd been shot. He got the heavy kid once more to his feet, clamped Nish's gloves to the back of the chair, and told him to skate using the chair for support.

Nish took a stride, and, instead of falling once again, the chair kept him upright. He took another stride, and the chair slid with him. Mr. Lindsay gathered up Nish's stick and followed as Nish and the chair made their way across the ice.

Most of the kids were laughing. Sarah took her stick and hit it hard on the ice, then again. Dmitri followed suit, and soon all the kids were banging their sticks on the ice in a salute as skater and chair moved toward them and Nish attempted to stop.

It didn't work. His feet went out from under him. The chair flew away and slid into the boards. Nish lay flat on his back, breathing hard, his wet red face glistening behind the cage.

"Your star has arrived," he announced.

FIRST THE FIRE ALARM WENT OFF AT LORD
Stanley Public School, then sirens could be heard,
growing louder as they screamed down Main Street,
all but drowning out the announcement from the
office over the intercom: "*Teachers will evacuate their
classes in an orderly fashion. There is no need to panic, but
classes should be moved quickly into the schoolyard according to planned routes.*"

Travis had been sitting at the art table, drawing
a huge picture of his first hockey practice. He had
Sarah with her ponytail sticking out the back of
her helmet. He had little Jeremy all but unable to
move in his big goaltending equipment. He had
himself flying about the ice with his stick raised
over the puck for a shot. And he had Nish, the
self-titled *star*, lying flat on his back beside the
stacking chair, a fountain of tears bursting almost
to the rafters, and his face crayoned a deep fire-
engine red.

41

Now there was a real fire engine pulling into the schoolyard – only this one was a bright, shiny yellow.

Miss Robinson hurried to line them up before counting heads: ". . . eleven, twelve, thirteen, fourteen, fifteen – *Wayne! Stay where you are!* – sixteen, seventeen . . ."

"What's going on?" little Simon squeaked.

Miss Robinson put her finger to her mouth to shush him and continued her count: ". . . eighteen, nineteen, twenty. Good, all here! Let's go now! Follow me, class!"

With Miss Robinson leading the way, the kindergarten class hurried to the doors leading out into the schoolyard. At the exit, Miss Robinson stepped to the side and tapped heads as the children passed, making sure she had all twenty of her students accounted for and safely out. Once they were all outside, she ushered the class to the far side of the schoolyard, where the kids took shelter from the sun under several large maple trees.

"*Look!*" Simon shouted, pointing high.

Travis looked up and saw several fire fighters – all dressed in slick yellow, two of them with oxygen masks on – working their way along the roof of the school building toward the chimney. There was no smoke coming from it – but then, why would there be? It was a hot early-September day. The furnace wouldn't be on.

Another man came up the ladder behind the fire fighters. He was carrying what looked like a cage; it was similar to the one Travis's grandmother kept for transporting her cat to and from the cottage. The man also had a net on the end of a long pole.

The schoolyard had filled up now, with hundreds of kids watching the drama take place on the rooftop. The fire fighters wearing the oxygen masks were working on the chimney, using crowbars to break away a covering. Once they were done, the man carrying the cage took over and began working his net down into the chimney.

"What's going on?" Sarah asked Miss Robinson. Miss Robinson shook her head. She didn't know.

Finally, the man pulled his net up and out. It contained something dark, almost black.

"It's a bomb," announced Nish as if he had known all along.

"*A bomb!*" shouted Derek.

Some of the other kids screamed. Little Simon looked like he was starting to cry.

"It's *not* a bomb!" Miss Robinson scolded Nish. "It's an animal or a bird or something."

The kids were fascinated. The man with the net carefully removed whatever it was from the net, examined it, and placed it cautiously into the cage before making his way back to the ladder.

One of the fire fighters on the roof, an older man with a different sort of cap – the captain, Travis figured – formed a megaphone with his hands and shouted down at the watching crowd. "*You can all return to your classes!*" he yelled. "*The alarm is over. Please return now to the school!*"

Nish edged up to Sarah and Travis. "That was fun," he mumbled, as the kindergarten class made its way back to the school. "I'm gonna have to remember that trick."

Sarah turned on him. "*What* trick? That was no trick – it was an animal in distress."

"Hey," Nish countered. "It got us outa school, didn't it?"

"You're sick," Sarah said, near tears. "How do you know whatever it is wasn't killed?"

"All I know is I'm not in school," Nish said. "I don't care about anything else."

"You're pathetic!" Sarah said, gritting her teeth.

Nish smiled a choirboy-like smile. "You'll learn to appreciate me," he said. "It'll just take time."

"If it takes forever, I'll never appreciate you, pal," Sarah said, moving on.

Travis hurried to keep up. He was delighted. Sarah was coming around to his way of thinking about this wretched red-faced idiot they'd been saddled with. But when he caught up to her, he saw she was quietly smiling to herself.

"What's so funny?" Travis asked.

"*He* is."

"He's a jerk."

"Maybe he is. But as I said, he makes things interesting. I may even get to 'appreciate' him one day."

Now it was Travis's turn to shake his head. Had Sarah lost her mind? *Appreciate* Nish? *Appreciate* the stupid, fat, red-faced kid who thought mooning school buses and finding dead animals down chimneys was good fun?

What was wrong with her?

9

TRAVIS HAD HEARD THE SOUND OF CRUNCHING bones before. He had snapped dry turkey wishbones at Thanksgiving, and he had heard a similar sound on those rare occasions when his family had lobster for dinner and his father helped him crack through the shells.

But he had never heard a sound like this. Not when the bones belonged to something still living, still struggling to escape. When the jaws closed on it, a skull crunched, like one of those walnuts his grandfather loved to crack open at Christmas. How could something so little be so powerful? Travis wondered.

It was the morning after the fire engine had arrived at Lord Stanley Public School. The kindergarten class had arrived to the sound of a pounding hammer as Mr. Greeley, the janitor, put the finishing touches to a large new cage that was dominating Miss Robinson's nature club.

The new cage completed, Mr. Greeley checked

the wire, adjusted the small sliding doorway, glued in a couple of perches along the back wall, and then stepped back as if expecting the small children watching to burst into spontaneous applause.

Travis really did feel like clapping. It was a wonderful cage. Mr. Greeley had built it of scraps of wood and chicken wire, but it was a work of art — every detail was perfect, and the cage stood strong and square in the centre of the classroom floor. But what was it for?

That question was soon answered. After Mr. Greeley had finished his work, the principal came in with two other people, a man and a woman. Travis recognized the man; he had carried the cage and the net to the chimney the day before. He had placed whatever it was he dragged out of the chimney in the cage and taken it down the ladder.

The woman was in uniform. She looked something like a police officer, but she wasn't. Her uniform was light green and had police-like badges on it, except the badges showed a green tree and the symbol for the province of Ontario, a single trillium plant in full white bloom.

"This is Mr. Stemkowski," the principal said, turning to the man. "He's the one who rescued the bird yesterday from our chimney."

So, Travis thought, it had been a bird. And if the principal said it was "rescued," it must be alive.

Mr. Stemkowski simply nodded and then turned to introduce the woman in uniform. "And this is Ms. Han. She's a conservation officer with the provincial department of natural resources."

"Hi, kids," Ms. Han said. She smiled one of those smiles that should come with a laugh track.

"What this is all about, children," the principal began, "is that we have an injured bird on our hands. Miss Robinson has kindly volunteered her nature club as a place where the bird might be cared for while it recovers. But if we go ahead with this, it is going to have to involve each and every one of you. Is that clear?"

The kindergarten class cheered as one. This was *exciting*. They were going to help "rescue" a wild animal!

"This bird is an owl," the principal continued. "It's a small one, not fully grown, and it's going to need some very special care if we're going to return it successfully to the wild. Are we all on for this?"

The class cheered again.

"The bird has one injured wing," said Mr. Stemkowski. "It's not broken, but it will take some time to heal. Ms. Han, here, will explain more."

"Owls are night creatures," said Ms. Han. "During the day, it will likely stay inside the small box your janitor has built inside this cage, so you won't see all that much of it. But at night it will want to fly and hunt, so we must always keep the cage door latched. And since it won't be able to hunt in this room – unless, of course, it likes to eat little kindergarteners" – the kids screamed in mock terror – "then we're going to have to keep it fed."

"I'll share my lunch," offered Fahd.

Ms. Han smiled. "No peanut butter sandwiches for this guy," she said. "That's why I'm here. I work with birds in the wild, and if you are going to return rescued birds to the wild, you have to keep feeding that bird the same diet it would encounter if left alone in the woods."

"Acorns?" the kid called Data asked.

"Grass?" offered Gordie.

"Mushrooms?"

Ms. Han smiled and shook her head at each suggestion. "In a moment, I'll show you," she said. "But you're all going to have to agree to this or else we can't do it."

With that, Mr. Stemkowski and Ms. Han stepped outside the classroom for a second, then returned carrying two boxes. Ms. Han set hers on the floor, put on what looked like very thick work gloves, then lifted the lid off the box Mr. Stemkowski was holding and reached in. When she drew her hands out, the kids squealed in delight.

"He's sooooooooooo cute," said Jennie.

What Ms. Han had in her heavily gloved hand

was a small owl. It seemed dazed and frightened. "I can feel his heart pounding," said Ms. Han. "It's going a million times a minute."

The bird was looking about anxiously. Its head seemed to turn as if on a swivel. And its yellow eyes were large and demanding – as though it were asking each one of the kids who they were, and what, exactly, they were doing.

The owl made no effort to bite into Ms. Han's gloves, but she still handled it very carefully, as if expecting that at any point the bird might attack. She lifted the doorway to the new cage and set the bird gently on one of the perches, waiting for it to wrap its talons around the perch and balance itself.

"He's beautiful!" whispered Sarah, almost breathless.

Ms. Han then went to the other box and opened it. Inside was a cage with fine wire mesh and a small trap door.

"They're alive!" shouted Simon.

"Owls eat live food," said Ms. Han. "You're going to have to get used to this. They eat field mice and shrews and moles. Is everyone still sure they want to go ahead with this project?"

"*Yessss!*" the class shouted as one.

Ms. Han slipped her gloved hand into the little cage and pulled it out holding a small field mouse. The little creature squirmed and tried to bite through the heavy gloves.

"Ahhh," said Liz. "Cute!"

"It's not about being 'cute,'" Ms. Han said, somewhat sternly. "It's about food."

With this, she opened the larger cage and pushed the panicking, wiggling mouse toward the owl, who eyed it suspiciously with those big, angry eyes.

Then, in an instant, the owl had chomped the mouse's head off.

And that was when Nish went down.

Travis had looked across at Nish when he heard a rather inappropriate giggle bubble up inside the Nincompoop, and he'd watched as the usual red colour had drained out of Nish's face as rapidly as if a tap had been opened below.

Down went Nish in a faint, his eyes rolling back in his head.

"Maybe this isn't such a good idea," the principal said, as she hurried to check on the collapsed boy.

"*Nooooo!*" said the kids.

"We want to do it!" said Simon.

Miss Robinson was fanning Nish's face. His eyes had stopped fluttering and he was staring up now. He shook it off, and Miss Robinson helped him to his knees, where he stayed, breathing regularly and trying to gain control of himself again.

"I think it will be fine," said Miss Robinson in a low voice. "It's going to be very educational for them."

"*Yeah!*" cheered Derek and Fahd.

"If you're going to do it," Ms. Han said, "you'll have to get used to this. The owl will eat four or five of these little creatures a day, and he will only eat them live. Otherwise, the owl dies. This is the way it is in nature, and this is the way it will have to be in the classroom if this is to work. Now you've seen what is involved, what do you have to say?"

The kindergarten class cheered its approval. Nish was back on his feet now, and, still white as a ghost, he meekly clapped his hands together.

"Okay, then?" Ms. Han said. "Any questions?"

"What sort of owl is it?" Fahd asked.

Ms. Han smiled at the question, pleased that the children were showing such interest in nature.

"He's a screech owl," she said.

She placed a wiggling black shrew in the cage this time, and the owl, eyes blinking, turned and chomped into it, bones crunching, fur flying.

"I think I'm gonna hurl," said a very weak voice from the side. And down went Nish again . . .

10

IT WAS THANKSGIVING.

School so far had been great. Each morning, Travis walked with Sarah, now his best friend. They still picked up Nish at the corner, but Nish at least was no longer mooning school buses. Perhaps it was because the weather had turned colder. Perhaps it was because he was smartening up. The chubby little kid was becoming almost bearable.

But not totally. Travis couldn't imagine ever coming around completely in his opinion of the chubby red-faced kid with the big mouth.

The little screech owl was holding its own. It ate more every day – the kids were now used to the crunching sounds – and had grown significantly larger. Ms. Han had returned from time to time to make sure the little bird was being cared for properly and was getting better. It was her opinion that the owl was a juvenile – sort of a teenager in bird terms – and had been out on his own and simply become lost. For whatever reason, likely because he saw it as a handy shelter, he had crawled into the school chimney and become stuck.

The class had even named the little bird. They had all been allowed to make suggestions and then held a vote. The result had been decisive:

Sidney: 12 votes
Crunchy: 3 votes
Screechy: 2 votes
Chimney: 2 votes
Wayne: 1 vote

Miss Robinson had insisted the vote be secret, but no one needed to ask who voted for "Wayne." Nish's beet red face gave that away. Who would ever name a pet after himself? Travis wondered. Well, Nish would. But then, Travis had to remind himself that Sidney wasn't a pet. He was a creature of the wild, and he would have to be returned to the wild as soon as he had recovered enough to strike out again on his own.

There was no more fainting, by Nish or anyone else. Some of the youngsters had been alarmed by the feeding of live mice and other small creatures to the owl, but after Ms. Han came back for a second visit and gave them a video presentation, they knew far more about the life and habits of the little screech owl.

When little Simon Milliken asked about the possibility of feeding the owl birdseed or kibble or something else that would spare the little mice, he was told that while the screech owl would eat a variety of other things, such as insects, live meat was necessary for two reasons. One, it was the main diet of the little owls. And two, if they got him eating only sunflower seeds and chopped vegetables, he would eventually become so dependent on being supplied such food that they would never be able to return him to the wild.

"Besides," Ms. Han said, "who here eats at McDonald's?" Little hands went up all around the classroom. Nish put up both his hands and pumped his fists. "Well, what do you think you're eating – hamburgers made of modelling clay?"

"Tastes like it sometimes!" Jesse giggled. "My parents won't eat there."

Ms. Han smiled. "Are you vegetarian?"

"No, we're Cree," Jesse answered.

Miss Robinson, who'd been sipping tea at her desk, almost spat a mouthful over the report cards she'd been working on.

Ms. Han looked puzzled. "Jesse's family comes from Waskaganish in Northern Quebec," Miss Robinson explained. "The Highboys are Crees from James Bay."

"Ah," said Ms. Han, "then tell us, Jesse, what you *do* like to eat if it's not McDonald's."

"We like feasts," said Jesse. "Whitefish, beaver, caribou, sometimes seal. My own favourite is moose nostrils."

Now it was Nish's turn to burst out. "*Moose nostrils? I'm gonna hurl!*"

Jesse was defiant. "They're good," he said. "Better than bacon."

"But this is exactly my point," said a delighted Ms. Han. "Everyone has a different diet. Jesse's family likes wild meat – 'game,' we call it – because that's what they have eaten there for thousands of years. Nish's family likes McDonald's."

"Double cheeseburgers, specifically," Nish added.

"Looks like you've had a few too many of them!" Sarah cracked and everyone else laughed. Nish stuck out his tongue at her.

"All right, children," Miss Robinson interrupted. "None of that. You listen to Ms. Han."

"And Sidney is no different," Ms. Han continued. "His family has always hunted and eaten mice and shrews and moles. And if we don't keep him on that diet, he will forget how to hunt and not know what to do once we take him back to his real home."

Nish raised his hand to ask a question. Travis had never seen Nish ask anything before.

"Then why don't we stop feeding him the mice so his diet will change," Nish said when Ms. Han acknowledged him. "That way, we can keep Sidney forever."

Some of the kids cheered. But Ms. Han shook her head immediately. "No," she said, "it wouldn't be right. Sidney is a wild creature and should live in the wild. How would *you* like to be kept in a cage for the rest of your life?"

Sarah answered instead. "Why don't you ask *us* if Nish should be kept in a cage?"

"*Children!*" Miss Robinson shouted over the laughter.

BEGINNERS HOCKEY HAD CHANGED DRAMATICALLY.
They were all coming along well under the guidance of Mr. Dillinger. Even Nish had moved beyond his ridiculous chair and was skating on his own, though he was still falling and sometimes refused to get up. Mr. Dillinger would just leave him lying there until Nish made up his own mind to rejoin the practice. One time, Mr. Dillinger even pushed Nish off into a corner as if he were some snow that had gotten in the way and had to be scraped to the side. Nish didn't seem to mind. He curled into a ball as Mr. Dillinger pushed him aside with his stick and slid happily into the corner, where he lay sucking his thumb and, once in a while, letting out a tiny whimper.

Travis decided he'd rather have nothing to do with Nish at hockey practice. He would still walk to school with him each day, but he would avoid him as much as possible on the ice – not that this was a difficult thing to do when Nish was curled up in a corner as if he'd decided to have a nap in the middle of everything.

Sarah and Travis were leading the group in abilities. They were the two best skaters, but the little blond kid with the funny name – Dmitri – was quickly catching up. In fact, Travis thought, if they had a race, Dmitri might win. He might not look as graceful as Sarah, might not look as much a hockey player as Travis did, but when those little legs began to skitter like a water bug, Dmitri flew down the ice.

Mr. Dillinger was a nice coach, but as Travis's dad rather carefully put it on the drive home after one Saturday morning practice, there wasn't much evidence that Mr. Dillinger had played as a youngster. That was just a polite way, Travis knew, of saying Mr. Dillinger didn't know the game.

Mr. Lindsay had helped out, and knew what he was doing, but he was travelling a great deal for work these days and found it difficult to make more than half the practices.

Travis had a very distinct memory of one practice where Mr. Dillinger had them doing a passing drill and nothing seemed to be working out. Mr. Dillinger had them stand across the ice from each other and just push the puck back and forth. Some of the kids were bored, some, like Nish, just fell down and stopped trying.

Mr. Lindsay had been away that week, and one of the men around the arena had come onto the ice in his winter boots and set things up for Mr. Dillinger. Travis had seen this man about the place before. He was thickly built, strong rather than fat. He had what you might call a crew cut, or a brush cut, but his hair looked like it had been cut by a riding mower rather than a pair of scissors. It also looked more like fur than hair. He had a broken nose, much like Terrible Ted Lindsay's crooked nose in some of the old family photographs Mr. Lindsay had of his famous hockey cousin. And, most noticeable of all, he walked with a limp.

Travis at first felt sorry for the man. When he came out on the ice, he had a hard time moving on the slippery surface, but once he took the stick and whistle from poor befuddled Mr. Dillinger, it seemed like he was standing out there in full NHL equipment during a warm-up.

The man had the kids divide into two groups and go to the corners. He then sent them out, one by one, to skate along the boards then sweep back at the blue line in a long curl to come toward the net and be given a pass for a shot. The pass would come from one of the kids on the opposite side, and next time it would alternate, with the kids who had given the pass now skating out and curling and coming in to take a shot. With each shot, the man had the two goalies switch so that one would take a shot, then the other.

Travis was astonished at how perfectly the drill worked and how almost . . . well . . . *beautiful* it was to watch. It was like a dance, with a pattern to it, and the kids got so excited about actually making a play that they were paying complete attention. Even Nish had crawled out of his nap corner to take part.

The man had used the two best skaters, Sarah and Travis, to demonstrate the drill. Travis was so nervous when he headed out and began curling at the blue line that he almost fell down, but when he turned and watched the man, standing in slippery winter boots, send a perfect, hard pass to him that landed exactly on the tape, Travis never felt so happy in his entire hockey life – short as it was at this point.

When his father returned from his business trip to Vancouver, Travis talked about the practice, and Mr. Lindsay had smiled and nodded.

"Muck," he said.

"What?"

"Muck Munro," Mr. Lindsay said.

"Muck? What kind of name is that?"

"It's a nickname," said Mr. Lindsay. "I don't know where he picked it up. Maybe because he was a rough-and-tough player and liked to 'muck' it up in the corners. He was probably the best player this little town ever produced."

"He played in the NHL?" Travis asked, suddenly very interested.

Mr. Lindsay shook his head. "Could have. Would have. He was Paul Henderson's teammate on the Hamilton Red Wings junior team. Everybody in Canada knows about Paul Henderson scoring that goal for Canada against the Soviets. But people said Muck was his equal or better."

"What happened?"

Mr. Lindsay sighed sadly. "Injury. Broke his leg in the Memorial Cup playoffs and some doctor set it wrong. The leg never came back, and Muck Munro's hockey days were over."

"Why doesn't he coach?"

"We've tried," Mr. Lindsay said. "I've tried and Don Dillinger has tried, and pretty well every person connected with minor hockey in this town has tried, but he keeps saying he'll think about it. You see him around the rink. He sharpens skates. He fixes the Zamboni when it breaks down. He's always first in line to help. But we've never been able to get him to coach."

"He'd be good," said Travis. "He knows what he's doing."

Mr. Lindsay smiled. "That he does. That he does."

12

THE ONLY ONE IN KINDERGARTEN CHANGING as dramatically as Sidney the screech owl was Wayne Nishikawa.

Travis was flabbergasted by the difference in the chubby little red-faced kid from down the street. He still thought of him as the Nincompoop from time to time, but less and less. Yes, Nish could do and say the most ridiculous things, but as the winter break approached he was definitely not as insufferable as he had been when school began back in the early fall.

Sarah put it all down to Sidney's influence. The little screech owl had been the star of the class from the very first day of its arrival. The feedings were now such a familiar event that no one really thought anymore about the fact that Sidney was eating live mice. And while Ms. Han and then Miss Robinson had handled the feedings for the first couple of weeks, these days Sidney was being waited on by virtually one person in the class: Nish. The kid who had fainted was now the one who was in charge of the feedings.

Ms. Han joked that Nish and the little owl had "bonded." She said to Nish, "Sidney thinks you're his *mother*," which caused the kindergarten class to howl with laughter and Nish to turn more shades of red than could be found in Miss Robinson's art cupboard.

But it was true. The little owl with the dancing eyes seemed to look for Nish deliberately. And once Sidney fixed his sight on Nish, he would become excited, knowing food was also on its way. The little owl would bound from one perch to the other and let out this bizarre sound that, the first time they heard it, sent chills through the class. "That's why they're called screech owls," Ms. Han had explained.

But now the screeching was as familiar as the school bells and the morning announcements. Nish would put on the feeding gloves — an old pair of work gloves supplied by Mr. Greeley, the janitor — and he'd catch one of the little mice and head for the cage and Sidney would go crazy with anticipation.

Nish acted like he'd been feeding wild birds all his life. His face had taken on a new look, Travis thought, sort of a weary, I-am-so-important look that Travis found slightly irritating but which Sarah found quite hilarious. At least it was a change from the phoney choir-boy look Nish put on whenever he was in trouble, or the whiny-baby look he put on when he fell on the ice during practice and Mr. Dillinger placed his hockey stick against his stomach and 'scraped' him off into a corner.

No, Nish was . . . *improving*. That was the only possible word for it. And he was clearly dedicated to Sidney.

Sidney himself was improving significantly. He was much bigger now – Ms. Han estimated he had gained 50 per cent more body weight since the day he'd been rescued. He was far more agile, leaping about wildly, especially when Nish approached the cage. And his damaged wing no longer hung awkwardly but folded against his body easily and comfortably, much as the good wing did.

The kids had even seen Sidney fly a bit – short little takeoffs and landings within the cage itself. Not really flying, but more than jumping. More like gliding.

Some of the youngsters wanted Sidney released in the classroom so they could see if he could really fly, but Miss Robinson insisted they wait for Ms. Han's next visit.

It was just as well, because Ms. Han was dead against the experiment. "It's too dangerous," she told them. "Birds don't know what windows are. Sidney would immediately try to fly out into the yard and would smash into the window. Besides, he's a night flyer. He wouldn't like trying to fly in daytime."

"We could turn off the lights and pull the curtains shut," little Simon Milliken suggested.

Ms. Han smiled. "We could, but you know what would happen?"

"No, what?"

"Sidney would go right back to what he is: a night hunter. First movement he saw, he'd attack. Say you sneezed, Simon. Sidney would nail your nose just like one of those mice we feed him. Would you like that?"

"*No way!*" Simon said, holding his nose.

"I think we're only a week or two away from releasing him back to the wild anyway," said Ms. Han. "He's recovered magnificently. What we'll do is take him from the class out to the woods one day and keep him caged until dark falls, then simply open up the cage and see what happens. Maybe Miss Robinson could arrange a field trip for the class so you could all watch."

Miss Robinson looked up from her desk and smiled. "That might be educational," she said. "I'll look into it."

The kids cheered. All, that is, except Nish.

Travis noticed Nish sinking into his seat, his chubby arms folded defiantly over his chest. Sarah, had seen the same thing. She looked at Travis and rolled her eyes. Travis understood without a word being spoken between them. Nish was going to lose his self-important role of Sidney's feeder. He was no longer going to be Sidney's "mother." He would just have to go back to being Nish, the crazy kid who mooned school buses and got himself caught in his zipper.

Travis smiled to himself. He was glad. He knew it was wrong to feel this way, but he was glad all the same.

13

THE BEST PART OF BEGINNERS HOCKEY, TRAVIS decided, was the scrimmages. Something happened the moment they stopped working on drills and stops and starts and turns and crossovers and instead just *played* the game.

He sensed Mr. Dillinger liked scrimmages best, too. In fact, Mr. Dillinger seemed *relieved* when the organized part of practice was over. The reason was painfully obvious to Sarah and Travis, who often discussed the situation on the way to school.

"Mr. Dillinger doesn't really know much about hockey, does he?" Sarah said one morning.

"We'll, we don't, either," said Travis.

"No, so he's fine right now. But one day we'll need a coach like your dad or that strange man who came out one day in his boots to show us something."

"Muck," Travis said.

"What?"

"'Muck,' that's what my dad calls him. Muck Munro, I think. He could have played in the NHL if he hadn't broken his leg."

"Well, whatever his name is, we'll need someone like that. Mr. Dillinger's got a good heart and works hard, but you can see he doesn't really know what to do in the drills."

"That's why he loves the scrimmages," Travis said.

"Don't we all?"

It was true. The moment Mr. Dillinger blew twice on his whistle, the kids started screaming and yelling with excitement. They knew it was time to play. Mr. Dillinger would line the kids up according to their sweaters – darks against lights – and then drop the puck at centre ice and skate, awkwardly, to the boards, where he would lean against them for support, watch, and smile. He clearly loved watching the kids scrimmage, too.

The moment that puck hit the ice, Travis felt more alive than he did doing anything else he had ever done. He could feel the excitement in himself and in all the other players. It was such a different feeling. It was as if once a game began, as opposed to a practice, Travis forgot all about his legs and skates, all about his stick and what he was supposed to do and he just reacted.

It was the most wonderful feeling. He would see the puck and simply will himself to go to it. His legs would fly and he'd have his stick reaching for the puck, but he never had to think about it or think about what would happen next. He just let it happen.

Dmitri was even faster during scrimmages than he was during practice. He seemed to click into a higher gear, shooting ahead past everyone else on the ice and, almost invariably, arriving first at the puck.

Sarah, of course, was all grace and style on the ice. She could carry the puck better than any of the others and pass it better than anyone, too.

Travis was starting to sense what sort of player he would become. He was quick, but not the fastest. He was a good passer, but not the best. He could shoot the puck in the net, but it was far more work for him than, say, for Dmitri, who was such a natural goal scorer that it seemed the puck ended up in the net every time he shot.

Jenny and Jeremy were becoming pretty good goalies. Both had trouble moving in their heavy equipment, but Jeremy was already working on his own version of the butterfly – going down on his knees and spreading the lower parts of his pads out to cover more of the lower part of the net – and Jenny was so good at cutting off the angles that it was hard to see how you could get a shot past her when she came out and challenged the shooter.

But they were still just little kids, and Travis knew that someone looking from the stands would see none of this. What they would see, instead, would look like a bunch of hornets buzzing around a small black dot, the puck, the whole cluster of them moving as one as the small black dot got slapped one way and then another.

Mr. Dillinger had only one rule for the scrimmages: no hitting.

It was only the third or fourth scrimmage when Nish decided to break that rule. Sarah had the puck. She was carrying it up over centre for the dark jersey side and she saw Dmitri streaking down the right-hand boards and led him with a perfect pass.

Dmitri had his head down to pick up the puck, and Nish had his big butt stuck out like a snow plough to catch poor Dmitri. Stick hit puck and Dmitri hit Nish at exactly the same time. Dmitri flew up onto Nish's back, did a flip in the air, and completed his unexpected somersault by landing perfectly on his skates and continuing dizzily down the ice until he crashed into the boards.

The puck stayed with Nish, the red-faced defender turning slowly to pick up the puck and starting to skate the other way despite the shrill calls of Mr. Dillinger's whistle. Mr. Dillinger's face was almost as red as Nish's.

"*What the heck was all that about?*" Mr. Dillinger screamed as he skated over, badly, to where Nish had stopped. Mr. Dillinger slipped and went down on one knee as he came to a stop himself.

Nish turned to face him, the choir-boy look perfectly composed on his face. "What do you mean?" he asked.

"*I said no hitting!*"

"He ran into me, sir . . ." Nish said.

Mr. Dillinger sputtered and seemed about to yell something else when he caught himself and settled down. He looked down the ice to where Dmitri, shaking his head like he'd run into a cobweb, was slowly coming back.

"That's why I turned," Nish continued. "I couldn't get out of his way in time, so I turned so no one would get hurt."

"He's lying," Sarah whispered in Travis's ear.

"I know," Travis whispered back. "He meant to do it."

"A *good* check," Sarah said with admiration.

Travis looked at her, blinking. How could she say that? They'd been told not to hit, and here was Nish, as usual, doing exactly what he'd been told not to do. And Sarah was almost applauding him. He would never understand these two.

• • •

They were undressing when Mr. Dillinger came into the room and looked around. Dmitri seemed fine now. The rest were taking off their jerseys and equipment and carefully putting away their stuff. All, that is, but Nish, who was simply dumping each piece of equipment into his bag as he took it off. Travis wondered if Nish's mother had ever washed any of his hockey equipment. He was halfway across the room, sitting between Sarah and Derek, and he thought he could smell Nish's sweaty stuff from here.

Mr. Dillinger cleared his throat. "Attention, kids," he began. "I have an announcement."

Everyone stopped what they were doing. Travis wondered if perhaps the coach was going to kick Nish off the team, but it turned out to be nothing like that at all.

Travis sat there in shock, shaking, as Mr. Dillinger continued: "The town of Tamarack has been chosen as a finalist in the CBC's contest to find the best, most enthusiastic 'hockey town' in the country – and you beginners have been invited to be part of the big day. You're going to be on national television!"

Mr. Dillinger waited for the cheers and screams to die down before telling them the details. "It'll be part of the TV show *Hockey Day in Canada*. During the winter break, you'll be going by bus to Toronto, where you'll be playing at the Air Canada Centre between the first and second period."

Travis felt a shiver run from his toes to the top of his head. He thought the hair on his head must be standing on end. He could hardly catch his breath.

"It will only be a five-minute game, but they'll show it on television. You'll be playing on the same ice as the Toronto Maple Leafs and the Pittsburgh Penguins, who will be playing that night."

"*The Leafs!*" Simon shouted.

"*The Pens!*" several other kids shouted.

Travis thought he was going to choke. He was going to be on *Hockey Day in Canada*.

He was going to play in the same rink that the Leafs and Penguins would be playing in.

In front of thousands of fans.

Millions of viewers.

Travis suddenly felt as dizzy as Dmitri had looked after Nish sent him flying in that somersault.

14

IT WAS SNOWING WHEN TRAVIS SET OUT FOR school: great, fat feathers of snow that seemed weightless as they drifted slowly down and landed on his coat and melted on his eyelashes. He had never seen snow so soft. If he swung his boot through the snow on the ground, it flew up like bath bubbles.

He met Sarah, as usual, at the corner. She was standing there with her mouth wide open, catching snowflakes. It looked like she was silently screaming at the clouds.

There would be no Nish this morning. For weeks now, the chubby little kid who once couldn't get to anything on time, who seemed to need his nap even in the middle of hockey practice, had been rising early and making it to school a half hour before everyone else. Mr. Greeley had even shown him where a key for the back door was kept hidden.

Sidney had totally changed Nish. He was no longer bragging about mooning school buses and quitting smoking at age four. The "new" Nish was prompt and happy and eager and more dedicated to the feeding and welfare of Sidney the screech owl than any of the other kids in kindergarten.

Each day, when Nish got to school, he would change Sidney's cage, put out fresh water, and feed the owl his first two mice of the day. By the time the other kids arrived, class could begin without the distraction of having to care first for the healing bird. Miss Robinson liked it this way; Ms. Han certainly approved of the arrangement; and Nish, it seemed, had never been happier.

Most afternoons, after school let out, Nish stayed behind just so he could be with Sidney then, too. He would feed him some more mice and make sure the owl had enough water for the night. For a kid who said he hated school, Nish was now spending more time there than anyone else in the class.

"He's completely changed," Sarah said, as they started on their way to school.

"Not completely," Travis argued. "He can still be a pain."

"He'll always be a pain – but that's what makes him so interesting. He's paying more attention in school. He's not exaggerating as much as more. And he's quickly becoming a pretty fair hockey player."

"He's too slow," Travis argued.

"I think you're *jealous* of him!" Sarah laughed.

"Am not!"

"Sure you are," she countered. "Every time I say anything about him, you have to knock him down. You're jealous."

Travis bit his lip rather than say more. He could feel his cheeks burning. He was surprised the big snowflakes landing on his face didn't vanish in a quick curl of steam.

Maybe Sarah was partly right: he *was* always putting Nish down. It bothered him that Nish got all the attention in the schoolyard. It still angered him that Nish had called him Zipper Boy when the true Zipper Boy had been Nish himself. And it had upset him at hockey practice when the other kids talked about Nish's amazing – and rather dirty – hip check on poor Dmitri.

Dmitri himself didn't seem at all bothered by it. By the time they cleared the dressing room, he had been laughing and slapping Nish on the back. And if Mr. Dillinger was upset, he hadn't shown it, joking about the check and telling the kids he'd have to put "back-up lights and a beeper" on that big butt of Nish's so there wouldn't be any more "accidents."

No one talked about what Travis had done at practice. He had caught a puck just right – okay, so it was up on its edge – and with a hard backhander he had put a shot over Jeremy's shoulder that rang off the crossbar so loudly everyone in the rink must have heard it. Only Sarah had said anything about it. Everyone else had been talking Nish, Nish, Nish . . .

I will stop being jealous, Travis told himself. I will start being nice to Nish . . . that Nincompoop.

"What's going on?" Sarah asked as she and Travis turned into the schoolyard. Kids from all classes were gathered around the kindergarten play area. Some were pointing. All were talking excitedly.

Travis was much too short to see past the crowd – especially the tall Grade Sixers – and couldn't understand what the kids were shouting about, so he and Sarah hurried in the kindergarten entrance.

The principal was standing at the classroom door, her arms folded in concern. Travis and Sarah slipped by without being noticed.

It was cold in the room, with a sharp winter draft coming from somewhere. Travis looked around, trying to take it all in at once. The large window had shattered as if a rock had gone through it, and all around the edges were sharp, jagged pieces. Mr. Greeley, the janitor, was plucking out the shards stuck in the frame. He had his heavy work gloves on and was using pliers to pull at the glass.

Miss Robinson was sitting on a tiny kindergarten chair in the nature club beside a distraught Nish, who was bawling his eyes out. His face was beet red. His eyes were squeezed shut. He was holding a

Kleenex, which was soaking wet and coming apart. Miss Robinson pulled a new tissue from a small pack and handed it to him. Nish took it without even opening his eyes and blew his nose — a loud, wet honk that almost caused Travis to giggle.

Except there was nothing funny about this. Nothing funny at all.

Nish was sobbing. Miss Robinson herself seemed on the verge of tears. Travis couldn't tell what Mr. Greeley was feeling as he carefully plucked out the remaining glass and dropped it, delicately, onto a large pile of glass that he had swept up at his feet.

The door to the owl's cage was open, swinging slightly.

SIDNEY WAS GONE AND NOWHERE TO BE FOUND.

"The door to the classroom was closed all night," Miss Robinson explained to the principal. "No way he could have got out into the hallway."

"Then there's no point in searching the school," said the principal.

Miss Robinson just shook her head. She still seemed on the verge of tears.

"It's pretty obvious where he went," Mr. Greeley said from his position at the window. "He wouldn't have known what glass was. Once he got free of the cage, he probably just flew into it straight-on. Looks to me like he burst through and away. There's no blood here that I can make out. And he sure ain't lying outside on the ground."

"Who left the cage door unlatched, then?" the principal asked.

Nish raised a hand, shaking. "M-m-me."

Miss Robinson stepped in quickly. "Wayne comes

early and stays late to care for Sidney. They're very close. It was an accident."

Mr. Greeley walked over to the cage and checked the doorway, jiggling it as he swung it back and forth on its hinges, checking and re-checking the small hook-and-eye latch that kept the door closed. "I'm the one to blame if anyone is," the janitor said. "This isn't a very safe latch. The bird might have been able to loosen it up by banging on it with his beak."

"It's my fault," Nish moaned. "*I lost Sidney . . .*"

Travis and Sarah looked at each other. They were both near tears themselves, and Nish's voice sounded like something that had come from a graveyard on a foggy night in some horror movie. They had never heard such sorrow, such sadness, such guilt.

"It's okay, Nish," Sarah said. "It's nobody's fault. Besides, look on the bright side: Sidney's *free* now. Just like we always planned."

If this was meant to comfort him, it had exactly the opposite effect. Nish listened to Sarah and then almost screamed as he began another long cry. It sounded worse than when he caught himself in his zipper.

Travis was about to roll his eyes at all the commotion, but then he stopped himself. Here he was, once again, coming down on poor Nish when he had just lost Sidney, his best friend in the world. Travis felt terrible all of a sudden. Nish was blaming himself, and, really, no one was to blame.

"There, there," Miss Robinson said, patting the back of Nish's head. "It's nobody's fault. No one got hurt. It's just a window, and Sidney is now off where he belongs. You go to the washroom, now, and clean up before class, okay?"

Nish, still sobbing, managed a weak "*o-okay*" as he got up from the chair and began shuffling toward the washroom. Travis had never seen a sadder sight in his life. Nish looked like he'd been punched in the stomach and kicked in the head.

His shoulders sagging, his feet dragging, his chest heaving with each sob, Nish stepped in behind the washroom door, closed it, and let out such a wail it sounded like he had caught his *neck* in his zipper.

Travis resisted trading looks with Sarah. He actually felt sorry for the big baby. He felt sad himself. His own eyes were stinging at the loss of little Sidney, even though he kept telling himself that what had happened was all right, that the screech owl had been on the verge of being returned to the wild anyway. Look on the bright side, Travis told himself. Obviously, Sidney's wing had healed.

Travis moved to the window. Mr. Greeley had swept up and was just finishing taping over the broken window to keep out the cold.

"That just about does her," said the janitor. "A few pieces outside to pick up and I'll have a new glass in here before noon."

Travis held the dustpan as Mr. Greeley swept the remaining glass into it. *So much glass*, Travis thought. *And so sharp!*

Sidney was a lucky bird to make it out without killing himself.

"I HAVE A FEW MORE DETAILS ABOUT OUR TRIP,"
Mr. Dillinger announced before the beginners went
onto the ice for their next session. "In the afternoon
we're going to be going to the Hockey Hall of Fame."

The kids cheered and hammered their sticks on
the dressing room floor.

"And we're going to attend the taping of one of
the *Hockey Night in Canada* intermission shows."

Again, cheering and stick-banging.

"And we're going to be playing against a group
of youngsters the same age as you guys, but who
have actually been playing as a team for some time
now. They're from Brantford, Wayne Gretzky's home
town, and they call themselves the Brantford 9.9s."

"What's that mean?" Fahd asked.

"No idea," shrugged Mr. Dillinger. "Maybe they
see themselves as a fraction of the Great One or
something – no doubt some adult named them and
nobody else gets it.

"Now," Mr. Dillinger continued, "this is just a very short little exhibition game, but we don't want to totally embarrass ourselves, do we?"

"Nish wouldn't mind!" Sarah shouted out to general laughter and a raspberry from Nish across the room.

Travis grinned. Nish was back. He was acting like his old self again after the shattering loss of Sidney the screech owl.

"Well," said Mr. Dillinger, "the rest of us would mind. So we have to make ourselves into a little team in time for *Hockey Day in Canada*. That's only two weeks away. We have to learn some position play, and we have to come up with some lines for the match. So what I've done is go out and hire some help." Mr. Dillinger smiled at his own little joke. "Well, not actually *pay* for help, but beg for it – just this one time only. And Mr. Munro – you'll remember he came out that day and taught you that shooting drill – has agreed to help us out for a few practices before we go."

"*Yes!*" shouted Data and Fahd together, hammering their sticks on the concrete floor.

"*Yes!*" shouted the others, following suit.

"Well!" Mr. Dillinger said, pretending to be hurt. "I guess I now know where I stand with you guys –"

"*Yay, Mr. D.!*" Sarah shouted, pounding her stick on the floor. The others all joined in until Mr.

Dillinger could only stand there and laugh, nervously running his hands through the thick fringe of brown hair that surrounded his balding head.

"Anyway," the coach continued, "we're going to have help for this little event, and I very much appreciate it. Mr. Munro will be handling the practices leading up to our Toronto trip."

At this point, Mr. Dillinger cleared his throat and stepped back toward the door. He opened it and called out, "Mr. Munro – could you come in for a moment?"

The door opened further and the temporary coach limped in. He was wearing old track pants and a very old hockey jacket that said "Hamilton Red Wings" across the chest and had the number 7 on one arm and "Left Wing" stitched halfway down the other arm.

"Guys," said Mr. Dillinger, "I want you to say hello to Mr. Munro."

"*Hello, Mr. Munro!*" the beginners called out as one.

"Muck," the man said. "You call me Muck, okay?"

"*Muck!*" the kids shouted back.

Travis was bewildered. He had never called a grown-up by his or her first name, let alone nickname. Even his dad had told Travis to call him "Mr. Lindsay" when on the ice so the other kids wouldn't think Travis was getting special treatment.

"Okay," Muck said. "Let's get out there and loosen up."

Cheering, sticks pounding, the kids made their way out onto the ice. Travis was first, as he liked to be, and immediately set out trying to leave a mark in the ice as he went through the first turn.

Sarah and then Dmitri flew past him, racing each other around the rink. He could see light dancing on their skate blades as they dug in hard and shoved off fast with each stride. He wondered if those skating beside him noticed his skate blades doing the same.

Derek caught up to him and whacked him in the seat of his hockey pants. "I can hardly wait!" Derek called.

"Me, too!" shouted Travis, and dug in hard for the next turn.

He was starting to lap some of the players, including Nish, who was dawdling as usual during the warm-up. Travis moved out to pass, digging in even deeper to impress Nish as he burst past.

And then he was airborne!

Travis flew through the air as if he'd been launched from a runway. He hadn't even seen Nish's stick come out and snake in between his legs, but he sure felt it as he tried for his next stride and his leg got caught. He hit the fresh, still-wet ice and seemed to pick up speed as he spun, helplessly, into the corner, where he crashed into the boards.

Nish skated by as if he hadn't even noticed. In fact, it seemed to Travis that Nish was deliberately looking in the other direction.

He rolled over, got onto his knees, and started to get up when he felt a tap on his pants. He got up just as Nish, having looped back, tapped him again.

"Sorry about that, buddy," Nish said. "You ran into my stick."

Travis doubted that. He was almost certain Nish had stuck his stick out deliberately to dump him. But he couldn't prove it. And no one else seemed interested in the slightest. "It's okay," Travis said, knocking off some of the water and starting to skate again.

"*Okay?*" he said to himself as he skated away. *What do I mean, "okay"? Okay that he dumped me? What a wimp I am. What a wimp!*

He was still cursing himself when he came out of the turn behind the net and saw Muck stepping out onto the ice. Muck had old hockey skates on. And very old hockey gloves. And a hockey stick the likes of which Travis had never before seen. *With a perfectly straight blade.*

He watched the temporary coach skate around for a bit, the stride so powerful and smooth on one side, yet cramped on the other. There was no doubt which was Muck's bad leg. It seemed shorter than the other, and sometimes Muck had to do a little hop-hop to right himself as he went into turns.

But still, the stride worked. Ice chips flew as Muck kicked off with his good leg. And the skates dug hard into the ice, making a sound like a sizzling frying pan as Muck did one final sharp turn and skated to centre ice, where he blew twice sharply on a whistle to bring everyone to him.

For Travis and the others, it was like making the leap from beginners class to the NHL in one morning session. They went from being little kids working on crossovers and skating around the circles to hockey players working with pucks and drills that seemed, at times, impossibly complicated, and at other times looked like they'd been designed by an artist.

Muck had them practising three-on-two rushes up the ice. He had the defence working on passing the puck across ice to each other before sending it out. He had them working on break-out patterns that would move the puck from their own end to centre ice.

He taught them how to space themselves in the opposition end. "We have three forwards," Muck said. "I want one high at all times and ready to jump into the slot for a shot. The other two will work the corners and watch for the high man to be free for that shot. You have time to pass. Don't panic, ever. And if the checking gets too close, you dump the puck in behind their net, always. The other player down low will be looking for that and can head there even before you dump it."

Travis wasn't sure he could follow all that. And the other kids seemed equally confused. But then Muck demonstrated what he wanted, and he explained everything so slowly, and so patiently, that everyone was able to follow.

Later in the practice, Muck began experimenting with lines. He put Derek and Gordie together with little Simon Milliken, and the three seemed to work well. He put Nish and Fahd back on defence.

He made Sarah his top centre and put Dmitri on the right side, because, as he said to Sarah, "You can send this guy in on breakaways all night long."

Muck was looking over the heads of the rest of the kids for a player to round out the top line. He reached over with his strange-looking stick and lightly tapped Travis on the top of the helmet. "You," Muck said. "What's your name?"

"Travis," Travis mumbled. He had never heard his voice so weak.

"You're the left winger. You're good with the puck, and you'll be the perfect trailer for these two speedsters."

Muck then had them work on carrying the puck down the ice as a line. Sarah liked to have the puck on her stick, but she also liked to pass when you weren't expecting it, so it took some time to iron things out, but soon the top line was moving quickly down the ice, back and forth, the puck moving fairly well among the three players.

Muck then turned to a scrimmage, using the lines and defence pairings he had come up with. This scrimmage was different, Travis thought instantly. Thanks to Muck's instructions, they were no longer trying to do everything on their own but were actually trying to make plays.

Travis's line was on with Nish and Fahd on defence, and Muck shot the puck hard down the ice and in back of the net, where Nish, skating faster than Travis had ever seen him go before, looped around and picked up the puck.

Nish sent the puck across ice to Fahd, just as Muck had told them to, and Fahd then chipped the puck off the boards to Travis, who at first thought he had lost it but was able to kick it up to his stick with his skate.

Travis saw Sarah cutting across, hammering her stick on the ice, and he passed – not as hard as he intended to, but enough to get there – and Sarah picked up the pass easily, stepping around Gordie Griffith, who was trying to check her.

Sarah instantly shot a pass across to the other side, where Dmitri was flying down the ice on the break-away Muck had said would happen. He took the puck, darted in on Jenny, and went to his backhand to lift the puck just over her pad.

It was, for Travis, the first time ever that he felt like a real hockey player.

Muck hammered his strange stick on the ice a few times to acknowledge the play and then sent the puck down for the other side to try their hand at a breakout. Gordie held onto the puck too long, though, and Sarah easily checked him. They tried again, and this time Gordie got the puck to Derek, who made it up over centre, where it seemed he ran into the boards long before he ran out of ice.

Nish.

Nish had simply placed himself and his big butt in Derek's way, and Derek had run smack into him and gone down like he'd been hit by a bus.

Muck blew the whistle. Twice. Hard.

Nish was going to be in trouble, Travis thought, as everyone skated over. There was supposed to be no body contact in beginners, and Nish had just levelled a player.

Nish had a look on his face that suggested he was preparing to get a lecture. He had his choirboy look on, but it instantly changed to surprise, and then a wide smile, as Muck began talking.

"I hope everyone saw that," Muck said.

They all murmured their agreement.

"What's the lesson here?" he asked.

"Don't bodycheck?" Fahd offered.

Muck gave him a withering look. "No. Not that. The lesson is one you may as well learn today, as you'll have to keep it in mind for as long as you play this game.

"*Keep. Your. Head. Up!*"

• • •

Nish was still smiling when they made it to the dressing room following the best practice they had ever had.

Mr. Dillinger was there, waiting. "One more thing, kids," Mr. Dillinger said. "We're playing a team with a name, and with dark blue jerseys, I've been told. We need to wear white. The hockey association has enough small whites for us to take to Toronto, and they are offering to put a small crest on if we like. Sound good?"

"*Yes!*" the players shouted and pounded their sticks.

"Well," said Mr. Dillinger. "We'll need a name, then. I was thinking Tamarack Tornadoes –"

"*No!*" Fahd shouted, then quickly added, "Sorry."

"Well, then, you come up with something."

They talked about it among themselves for a bit. Some suggestions, like the Penguins, the Leafs, the Senators, the Flames, were simply taken from the

NHL, and some, like the Shooters and the Pucksters, were made up on the spot.

"I have one," said Sarah, raising her hand.

"Okay now, shush up!" ordered Mr. Dillinger. "Let's hear what Sarah has to say."

"I think we should be called the Screech Owls," Sarah said.

Mr. Dillinger looked absolutely baffled.

"The Screech Owls," he said. "What kind of name is that?"

"The perfect name," said Sarah.

"Yes!" agreed Fahd.

"*The Screech Owls!*" shouted Liz and Jennie.

"*Yes!*"

"*Yes!*"

"*Yes!*"

Even Travis found himself shouting in agreement, though he would much have preferred the "Penguins," as they were his favourite team. But this was perfect. It would honour Sidney.

He looked across the dressing room at Nish, who was beaming like a tomato that had gone so ripe it was close to bursting.

THE EXCITEMENT WAS BUILDING FOR *HOCKEY Day in Canada* and the Screech Owls' trip to Toronto. Miss Robinson had run a logo contest in art class to see who could draw the best crest for the new white jerseys the little hockey team would be wearing, and Liz had won handily with a colourful drawing of a little brown screech owl standing on a puck.

Nish claimed it looked more like a bear than an owl, but no one paid him much attention. His own effort looked like a hot dog with wings.

Muck had given out the numbers to the players, simply plucking the new jerseys from their hangers and handing them over as he went around the room.

Travis had received number 7, Terrible Ted's old number with the Detroit Red Wings – and Muck's old number, he noted, when Muck had played for the junior Red Wings back in Hamilton.

Sarah got number 9, which pleased her. Jesse was handed number 10. Gordie got 11. Jeremy, the starting goalie, asked for and got number 1. And Nish, because he was so much bigger than the others, received the largest sweater in the stack, number 44.

The Screech Owls were a team. They had sweater numbers. They had a name. They had lines. All they lacked now was a game. They had never played one.

• • •

Mr. Lindsay noted one evening that Travis's wooden stick was beginning to show some wear around the heel. "You have to watch this," Mr. Lindsay said. "Water seeps in and the wood starts to go 'punky' on you – sticks aren't much good after that. We'll see about a new one tomorrow."

Travis could hardly believe all the good things that were happening to him. Perhaps, with luck, he'd get a composite stick this time. Not one of those sticks that his father complained cost more than their television set, but one of the cheaper composite ones like some of the other kids had. He was sure that with a stick like that he'd be able to shoot better – perhaps even raise the puck off the ice when he shot.

On Friday evening, Travis and his father went downtown to Canadian Tire to look for a stick. They checked out everything, from a cheap wooden stick that Mr. Lindsay said wouldn't last a game, to a lightweight composite that carried a price tag that made Mr. Lindsay suck in his breath as if he were in pain.

"Let's go down to the Home Hardware and see what's there," Mr. Lindsay suggested, not satisfied with the selection.

They got back in the car and headed for Main Street, where the smaller stores of Tamarack were located. Travis liked the downtown far better than the big-box mall out by the highway at the north end of town. He liked downtown because the stores there seemed less interested in selling than in visiting. People knew each other's names along Main Street. And there was a new store with new windows every few steps, not stores so massive that you had to drive from one to the other.

Travis was quickly learning the downtown Main Street stops by heart. There was the Bluebird Theatre, the jewellery store, a small meat market, a bakery, a newsstand, two restaurants, the hardware store, a pet store, a shoe store, a women's clothing store, a second-hand shop, the offices of the local weekly newspaper, and a grocery store.

Mr. Lindsay seemed more satisfied with the selection here, even if there weren't as many sticks to choose from. He didn't flinch at the prices, and, best of all, there was a whole section devoted to composite sticks for juniors. He had Travis try several different sticks and blades. Travis liked one that was electric blue in colour and had a slight curve to it.

"Muck has a perfectly straight stick," Travis told his father. "Ever see one?"

Mr. Lindsay laughed. "Ever *see* one? I played with one all my minor hockey days. No one had a curved stick then. There was a guy who played for Chicago Blackhawks, Stan Mikita, and he started tying rocks to his stick blade and soaking it in the bathtub for days. When he took it out of the tub, the blade was shaped like a banana. He and Bobby Hull, his teammate, started using the curves for slapshots, and pretty soon after that there wasn't a single goaltender in hockey not wearing a mask for protection."

"You mean goalies once didn't wear masks?" Travis asked.

"And players didn't wear helmets," Mr. Lindsay added.

"Couldn't anybody hoist?" Travis asked.

Mr. Lindsay just chuckled. "Yes, they could fire the puck then, too. It's surprising no one was killed. Glenn Hall once played 502 games in a row in goal, and never wore a goalie mask. You'd never see that happen today."

"He must have been scared," Travis said.

"Maybe so," said Mr. Lindsay. "They say he threw up before every single game he ever played. Said it was nerves, but maybe it was fear. Who knows? Here, try this one again . . ." Mr. Lindsay handed back the electric blue composite stick, and Travis pretended to take some shots with it.

"Like it?"

"I *love* it."

"Then let's get it."

Travis couldn't believe it – a composite stick, and a good one at that. With this stick, he'd be ten times the player he was before. He'd use this stick for years – maybe even right up until he got drafted into the NHL.

They paid for the stick, Mr. Lindsay and the cashier chatted a little about the storm warnings they'd been hearing all day, and then they headed back out onto Main Street to find their car and head for home.

Travis went out, turned left, and almost ran right into Nish and his mother coming out of the pet store.

Nish's face, usually beaming like a tail-light, was white as a ghost.

"Hi!" Travis said eagerly.

"H-hi . . ." Nish mumbled.

"Hello, Travis, how are you?" Nish's mother said.

"Just fine, Mrs. Nishikawa."

Travis's dad leaned forward, sticking out his right hand. "How do you do, Mrs. Nishikawa, I'm Travis's father."

As the two adults made their own introductions and began to discuss the weather, Travis turned back to Nish, who seemed remarkably nervous. "I didn't know you had any pets," Travis said. "What were you doing in the pet store?"

"Nothin'," Nish snapped. "Just looking. Maybe we'll get a puppy in the spring, my mom says. What kind of stick did you get?"

"Composite," Travis bragged. "It's a Laser. Not top of the line, but a good one. I love it."

"I'm getting one, too," said Nish. "Soon as we can save up."

The parents were still talking. Nish, keeping his purchase tight to his side, reached over with his free hand and pulled his mother's jacket.

"Let's go, Mom. Gotta get back."

Travis had never seen Nish so out of sorts. He seemed flustered, anxious to get going. He hadn't said what they'd been buying, but obviously they'd got something.

Travis tried to see into the bag that Nish was holding. But Nish, seeing Travis edge closer, wrapped a mitten tight over the top of the bag so nothing could be seen.

It was like he has a secret, Travis thought. Something he doesn't want me to know about. *But what?*

PERFECT.

The new stick was fantastic. It was so light, it was as if Travis held air in his hockey gloves. It had just enough whip in it to help him hoist the puck higher and harder than ever before. And every other kid on the team had noticed its beautiful electric blue colour and, Travis was sure, wished he or she had one just like it.

He was first on the ice for the new "Owls" next practice. His first shot on the empty net during warm-up went so high it pinged off the crossbar. Okay, so the puck was on its edge and lifting it was easy – but it was still a crossbar shot.

Travis loved the sound of the puck hitting steel. To him, it was the sweetest hockey sound of all. Better than a puck on boards. Better than the sounds of stickhandling. Better than the whoops and yells of the kids playing a game of scrimmage. Better, even, than being able to hear your skates sizzle on a hard corner turn on fresh ice.

He made a promise to himself. He would try, from that moment on, to hit the crossbar during every warm-up for good luck. Why not? Warm-ups weren't the game; they didn't count; and everyone would notice when little Travis Lindsay rang a shot off the crossbar.

He imagined himself ringing the puck off the crossbar in the first NHL game he ever played. He saw himself pinging one off the crossbar before the annual NHL all-star game where he was the starting left-winger. He could see himself hitting the crossbar in the warm-up to the seventh game of the Stanley Cup final – which he would win by scoring in overtime . . . The puck going in, of course, off the crossbar . . .

Muck's whistle brought Travis back to reality. Two quick bursts, and the Owls were all scurrying to join Muck at centre ice.

"We got a lot still to work on," Muck told the little Owls as they came to a stop, several of them falling, as they still had to master the simple turn of the blades that brought them to a quick halt. "Today I want a full scrimmage, darks against whites, lines together. I want to see how you work as a team."

The players cheered and machine-gunned their sticks on the ice at this announcement.

Sarah's line, with Travis and Dmitri, would start on one side, with Derek's line on the other. Once again, Nish and Fahd were back on defence.

Muck dropped the puck, and Sarah accidentally plucked it out of the air before it even struck the ice. Before Gordie Griffith could even react, she was off with the puck, moving in on Wilson and Data, who were playing defence for the darks.

Travis followed her. Sarah came in, forced the defence back, then dropped the puck between her skates for Travis.

It caught him off guard. He spun, picked up the loose puck and saw Dmitri out of the corner of his eye. Travis was on the backhand, though, with no time to turn to his forehand, so he let the pass go on the backhand – only to watch helplessly as it skittered away over the blue line, leaving his team offside and putting an end to the attack.

Muck's whistle shrieked a stop to the play.

Muck skated up to where Travis had messed up, kicked the puck toward Travis, and then handed his strange stick to Travis.

"Take it," Muck ordered. He reached out and took Travis's stick from him.

Muck's stick, by comparison, felt like it was made of lead. It was heavy as stone, and way, way too long.

"Try that same backhand pass now," Muck said.

Travis turned so he was again on the backhand. Muck signalled with Travis's electric blue stick for Dmitri to skate along the far boards, just as he had before, and Dmitri spun back over the line, turned, and came back in skating hard.

Travis looked down the long stick. It seemed to him that the blade was curved the *other* way, for a left-handed shot. But the blade wasn't curved in either direction – it was straight as a ruler. It looked to Travis as if the puck would just dribble off in the wrong direction if he tried a shot on his forehand.

But on the backhand, it was another story. Dmitri was moving fast, and Travis, choking up on Muck's long stick, tried his pass. The puck stayed hard to the blade until he released it, sliding fast and sure, right to the tape on Dmitri's stick.

"You see the difference?" Muck said.

Travis nodded.

"I know I'm not going to change the world," Muck said, "but if I can get you kids to respect the backhand I'll have done enough."

He took back his stick from Travis and held it out like a sword so everyone could see how straight the blade was. "This is how sticks used to be made," he said. "Some of the greatest players in the history of the game were as dangerous on the backhand as they were on the forehand. Today's players are afraid of backhand shots, so they lose pucks all the time trying to turn over to their forehand. It wastes time and loses possession. I can't stop you kids from having curves – I doubt you can even buy a straight stick anymore – but if this convinces you not to have *too much* of a curve, then maybe we'll see some backhand passes that connect one day. Okay?"

The Owls shouted out their agreement. Travis took his stick and marvelled again at its lightness. But he also realized that Muck was right. His next stick wouldn't have such a big curve to it.

Practice went well from that point on. The Owls already looked less like a bunch of hornets buzzing around a nest and more like a bunch of kids playing a real game of hockey.

Little things were starting to be noticed. Not just Dmitri's speed and Sarah's playmaking skills, but Derek's hard work and Data's good poke check and Jennie's sure glove hand.

Nish was also beginning to be noticed – most of all by Travis. In a matter of a few months, Nish had moved from the snivelling kid who lay whimpering on the ice to a kid who seemed to want to have the puck on his stick. Nish was very aggressive and very, very effective in his own end. He could trap the puck along the boards and then turn his big butt on a checker and end up coming out of the corner with the puck on his stick. He was a pretty decent stickhandler. And he skated with his head up, rather than down, so he could see where he might make a pass.

Twice Travis had broken across his own blue line only to be hit by a perfect blade-to-blade pass by Nish. One he lost, and one he kept, sending the puck ahead to Sarah, who dished off to Dmitri, and Dmitri scored on a nice *backhand*, which drew a flew slaps on the ice from the big uncurved stick of the temporary coach.

Sarah caught a ride home with Travis and his father, and she, obviously, had noticed the same thing about Nish.

"I think that big goof is already our best defence player," she laughed.

Mr. Lindsay agreed. "He's a natural."

"Don't tell *him* that," warned Travis. "He's already impossible."

"Well, there's no denying he's good," said Mr. Lindsay. "He sees the ice, and that's a gift you don't learn. Gordie Howe used to say, if you parted Wayne Gretzky's hair at the back, you'd probably find a third eye there. That's how well Gretzky saw the ice around him. Yet he never seemed to be looking at all."

Travis listened but didn't say anything. He was staring out the back window, watching the high snow banks slip by as his father drove and chattered on with Sarah about Nish.

Travis felt like he was still sweating from the practice. He put a hand to his forehead and felt heat, almost burning. He knew he was red without using the mirror to check.

He also knew what it was, and it only made him burn all the hotter. He was *jealous*.

TRAVIS WAS HAVING TROUBLE SLEEPING.

He thought it must be excitement about the upcoming trip to Toronto, but usually, when he thought about things to do with hockey, he fell asleep immediately. (And when he was really lucky, he dreamed about hockey.)

What was troubling him was Nish. It wasn't his own jealousy of Nish, his feeling that Nish was getting all the attention, but something else, something Travis couldn't quite put his finger on.

Nish had changed so dramatically from that first awful day, when he caught himself in his zipper and then later pretended it was Travis. He had gone from a whiner who said he hated to school to the kid who came early and stayed late to care for Sidney, the little Screech Owl. He had gone from the kid who needed a chair to keep him upright on the ice to the best defenceman on the team.

But now he had changed again. He was still not

walking to school with Sarah and Travis and still not walking home with them. Except now, each morning, he was coming in *late*, usually racing across the schoolyard to get into the kindergarten before the school bell went. And each afternoon he was gone the second the principal ended her announcement over the intercom and school was dismissed. Sarah and Travis would be putting on their winter boots as Nish shot past them out the door, not even explaining why he wouldn't be walking with them.

"Maybe his mom's sick," Sarah had suggested.

Travis didn't think so. He'd seen her downtown, and Mrs. Nishikawa and his mother had talked for a long time. Mrs. Nishikawa had said how busy Nish was with his new project.

But *what* project?

Travis tossed and turned in his bed. He kept thinking about how the little owl had changed Nish so dramatically, and how Nish, really, had never been the same since he'd become Sidney's "mother." Some of the changes were for the good. Some, he thought, were for the bad.

He kept thinking about Nish that morning the little owl escaped. He could see him sobbing uncontrollably in the chair as Miss Robinson tried to convince him it wasn't his fault the cage door had been left open.

He could see Nish making his way to the washroom, still bawling, as Mr. Greeley piled up the glass in the dust bin with Travis and Sarah's help before someone could cut themselves.

For a long time, Travis stared at the ceiling, blinking as if there were a strong light there beaming back down on him.

The glass, he kept thinking. The glass . . .

. . . and then he was asleep.

20

AGAIN, IT WAS JUST SARAH AND TRAVIS WALKING together to school. It was colder than it had been, too cold to snow, and the snow that had fallen earlier in the week crunched beneath their boots like they were walking on popcorn.

"Do you remember the broken window when Sidney got away?" Travis asked, the question forming a balloon of steam in front of his mouth.

"Of course," said Sarah.

"I was thinking, last night, that all the glass was *inside* – or at least most of it."

"Yeah, so? Sidney smashed into it from inside, remember?"

"Yeah, but wouldn't that cause the glass to fall outside?"

Sarah thought for a moment, her breath puffing through her nostrils as she stood there. "There was some outside, remember? Mr. Greeley went out to pick it up."

"Yeah, but not much," said Travis. "We helped clean up inside, almost all of it was there."

"I'm not sure what you're getting at," said Sarah.

"If the glass came down inside, then the window would have been hit from *outside*, wouldn't it?"

Sarah thought about it some more. "Yes, it would, I guess," she said, nodding. "Are you saying someone broke the window so Sidney could escape?"

"I don't know what I'm saying," Travis admitted. "Just that there's something very odd going on. Nish hasn't been the same since that day, you know."

Sarah laughed. "What's the 'same' about Nish. Every single day he's different. Every single hour is different with him."

"But he's gone very quiet, or haven't you noticed? He hardly talks to us at all, even at hockey, and we never walk to or from school with him anymore."

"Maybe he doesn't like us any longer."

"I think he's got a secret."

Sarah stopped dead this time. "What sort of secret?"

"I don't know. But he's hiding something."

Travis then told Sarah all about the encounter on Main Street when Travis and his father had gone to buy a hockey stick. Travis couldn't understand what

Nish was buying in the pet store that he wouldn't tell Travis about.

"Did he ever mention a pet?" Travis asked.

Sarah shook her head. "Not that I ever heard."

"He never said anything in class. No cat. In fact, I think he said he was allergic to cats. And no dog. No gerbil. No mice, even though he fainted the first time they fed one to Sidney. If he'd had mice as pets he would've said, wouldn't he?"

Sarah was thinking hard. "Let's *make* him walk home with us today," she said.

"What good will that do?" Travis asked.

"We'll just study him, see what we can find out."

Travis nodded. They had a deal.

• • •

"*Hey!*" Sarah shouted. "*Wait for us!*"

Nish stopped in his tracks at the door. Class was over, and already he was on the run. But Sarah's shout had caught him.

Travis could see Nish's face twist like someone had squeezed it.

"Gotta help my mom," he explained hurriedly. "She's expecting me."

"Don't worry," Sarah said. "We'll hurry. We'll get you home in time. We're *supposed* to walk together, you know."

"Yeah, I know," Nish conceded. "But I have to get back fast, okay?"

"Okay, okay – just hold up a sec and we'll be with you."

Sarah and Travis hurried into their boots and jackets, and the three burst out of the doors together and all but ran across the schoolyard to the street.

Travis had never seen Nish walk at such a pace. He hardly seemed related to the slow-moving, lazy Nish they had met the first time they all walked together to kindergarten.

"You know, Nish, we've been thinking," Sarah began, a bit breathless from the speed at which they were walking.

"What?"

"About the day Sidney escaped – remember it?"

"'Course I do."

"Travis noticed that the window seemed to have been broken from the outside rather than the inside."

"It was broken when we got there. How could you know?"

"Well," Travis said. "If the glass was mostly on the inside, it would have been broken from the outside. If it had been broken from the inside – like if Sidney had crashed into it, as we think happened – then the glass would have been mostly outside. But Sarah and

I helped Mr. Greeley clean up, and almost all the glass was on the inside."

"Maybe the wind broke it," said Nish, hurrying even faster.

"Why would it break just the one window?" Sarah countered. "Besides, I don't remember it being windy that day."

"Maybe you're wrong," Nish said. "Maybe there was more glass outside."

"I don't think so," said Travis. "I looked pretty closely."

"Well how should I know?" Nish snapped and picked up his pace again until he was nearly running.

"What gives, Nish?" Sarah asked, giggling. "You trying to get in shape or something before *Hockey Day in Canada*?"

"I told my mom I'd be home right after school. I'd be there already if you two hadn't held me up!"

Nish practically spat out this last bit and then broke into a full run, his chubby legs taking him fast down the street beneath the elms and his school backpack swaying on his back.

Sarah and Travis moved to keep up, but then Sarah stopped abruptly. "Let him go," she said to Travis. "This is stupid!"

Travis, too, came to a stop. Nish was already rounding the corner up ahead and disappearing out of sight.

"What was all that about?" Travis asked.

"I have no idea," Sarah said, smiling, "but we'll find out."

Travis looked at her, his face wrinkling. "How?"

"Simple," Sarah said. "We slow down. We give him time to get home . . . and then we *call* on him."

SARAH AND TRAVIS WASTED SOME TIME BY going to the park and taking a few turns on the slide, then trying to walk along the plastic balance beam next to the climbing bars.

If anyone happened to see them, they would just think it was a couple of little kids dawdling on the way home from school. No one would know they were on a mission to find out exactly what was causing Nish to race home after school each day and then be late for school each next morning.

"Okay," Sarah said. "Let's go."

They picked up their backpacks and made the same turn onto the same street that, fifteen minutes earlier, Nish had taken. They walked slowly up to his house and stood at the door.

"What're we going to ask?" said Travis.

"If Nish can come out and play," Sarah said. "What could be simpler?"

"I don't know," Travis said. "You do the talking."

Sarah pushed the buzzer. Nothing happened. She pushed it again, and Travis could hear the sound of heels on a hardwood floor. Someone was coming.

The door opened and Mrs. Nishikawa stared out, and then smiled widely. "Sarah! Travis! Hello, you two. Where have you both been hiding these days? I never see you."

"Is Wayne here, Mrs. Nishikawa?" Sarah asked, careful to use Nish's real name in front of his mother.

"Of course," Mrs. Nishikawa smiled. "He's downstairs feeding that silly bird of his."

Sarah looked at Travis, her eyes growing as wide as . . . well . . . *an owl.*

Nish had been found out.

Mrs. Nishikawa had known nothing of what had happened at school. She thought the little bird had been given to Nish to keep as a pet. He told her the owl had been unable to recover well enough to fly and Miss Robinson had decided to send it home with the one youngster the owl was closest to. And that, of course, was Nish.

The truth only came out when Mrs. Nishikawa left them in the basement and went back upstairs to her kitchen, allowing Travis and Sarah to grill their red-faced little friend, the owl kidnapper.

"Why did you do it?" Sarah wanted to know.

Nish was twisting his hands and avoiding eye contact, but he couldn't avoid the question. "I-I couldn't stand the idea of Sidney being sent out into the wild," he said, clearly flustered. "He would have died if we'd let him go like Ms. Han wanted."

"How do you know that? She's the expert, not you."

"I could see it in Sidney's eyes. He was scared to be let free again."

"But how did he end up here?" Travis asked. "How did you get him out without anyone knowing?"

Nish didn't seem to want to talk about it. He just sat, wringing his hands, his big face turning redder and redder. His cheeks clammed over with sweat as he worked his way through what he would say. Finally, Nish sighed deeply and told them what had happened.

"It wasn't hard," he said. "In fact, it was really very easy. I took him in the evening, after his last feeding of the day. I saw that there was no one around – Miss Robinson had already gone home, and Mr. Greeley was sweeping the halls – so I put Sidney in my coat and smuggled him out and home. I left the cage door open so it would look like he'd escaped.

"I went back after dark with my hockey stick and reached up and hammered the heel of the stick through the window so it would look like Sidney had crashed through."

"Which is exactly what Ms. Han had said he would do if he got out of the cage," Sarah suggested.

Nish nodded. He was crying now, big drops forming in his eyes, rolling down his burning cheeks, and dropping onto his shirt.

"That explains how the glass was on the inside," said Travis. "I thought maybe someone had thrown a rock through the window – but we would have found the rock in the classroom, so it couldn't have been that. I never thought about a hockey stick."

"I told my mom that the bird had been given to me to care for. She was the one who bought this cage. She paid for the mice I had to buy."

"*The pet store!*" Travis almost shouted. "That's why you wouldn't show me what you'd bought. You had mice there for feeding Sidney!"

Nish nodded, his chubby chest heaving. "Miss Robinson told me she got the mice each week at the downtown pet shop. They sell them for people to feed to their pet snakes. Are you going to tell on me?"

"The bird isn't yours," Sarah said. "We have to take him back and have Ms. Han check him out."

"What about my mom?" Nish asked, the tears really beginning to roll. "She doesn't have to know, does she? I mean, she's the one who bought the cage. She's the one who paid for the feed. She thinks I've done something good by taking care of Sidney. She thinks Sidney has been good for me . . ."

Sarah was nodding, but also frowning. Of that there could be no dispute – Sidney had been good for Nish. Very good. But what Nish had done was wrong. And the bird would need to go back.

Sarah and Travis exchanged glances. "Okay," Sarah said. "You simply tell your mom you think Sidney is well enough now to be released back into the wild. You tell her Sidney has to go back to school so Ms. Han can check him out and see if you're right. You tell her you'll take him back tomorrow."

Nish looked up weakly. "Tomorrow?" he squeaked.

"Tomorrow," Sarah insisted. "We'll come by and pick you up."

Nish nodded. He was crying openly now.

Travis thought he understood why. Part of it was getting caught. Part was having to give Sidney up. And part, knowing Nish, was pure relief at not having to tell his mother.

FIRST THING IN THE MORNING, SARAH AND Travis knocked on Nish's front door. It opened immediately. Nish was there, dressed in his winter jacket and holding a large bag containing a blanket and, inside the blanket, Sidney.

Mrs. Nishikawa was also there. She seemed sad to see the little bird go, but obviously she had been told, and had bought Nish's tale of how the time had come for the owl to leave her basement.

"You take care, little bird," Mrs. Nishikawa said, patting the bag gently. "And good luck!"

The three kids set out. Travis had offered to carry Nish's backpack so Nish could pay more attention to the bag holding Sidney.

Nish was now in no hurry. He seemed to be dragging his feet, trying to preserve every possible moment with his beloved owl. But the other two kept pressing.

"Are you sure he can breathe in there?" Sarah said at one point.

"He's okay."

"Let me just have a peek," Sarah said.

Nish seemed grateful for the chance to look in. They gathered around the bag, Nish carefully moved the wool blanket to the side, and they found themselves looking in on a very surprised, trembling little bird.

A trembling little bird that instantly became a wild little bird, thrashing to get out.

"*Watch out!*" Sarah screamed. But it was too late. Sidney twisted and climbed frantically with his claws and, in an instant, was free of the wool blanket and the bag and was shooting straight up into the sky.

"NNNNOOOOOOOOOOO!!!!" Nish screamed.

"Come back!" Travis yelled, but he knew there was no use. Sidney flew up into the bare branches of one of the elms and perched there, looking back down on the kids.

Nish seemed hopeful. "*Atta boy, Sidney!*" he shouted up. "C'mon back down here right now. You'll *freeze!*"

"Screech owls are fine outside in winter," Sarah said. "He'll be all right."

After one last look below, and almost as if he'd heard Sarah say he'd be okay, Sidney took off again and, looping through the branches, was soon lost from sight.

"*No-no-no-no-no!*" Nish moaned. "What're we gonna do now?"

"Nothing," Sarah said.

"*Nothing?*" Travis asked.

"*Nothing?*" a surprised Nish repeated.

"Nothing," Sarah said. "What happened to Sidney, as far as Miss Robinson and Mr. Greeley and Ms. Han and all the other kids know?"

"He escaped," said Travis.

"Exactly," Sarah said. "And what just happened now?"

"He . . . es-es-caped," Nish stuttered.

"Exactly," said Sarah. "So now, everything is exactly the way everybody thinks it is, right?"

Travis wasn't so sure. "Yes, but . . ."

"C'mon, Trav," Sarah said. "Sidney is all right. He's back in his own world. And Nish doesn't need any more trouble, does he?"

"What about the broken window?" Travis said. "That was wrong."

"He knows it was wrong," Sarah said. "Don't you, Nish?"

"I'll never do anything bad again, as long as I live," Nish promised, the tears again rolling down his cheek.

"I doubt that very much," said Sarah, "but let's just leave it. Nish has learned his lesson, I think."

Nish seemed stuck for words. He swallowed. He wiped his red eyes.

"You guys would do that for me?" he asked.

"We're teammates," Sarah said, smiling. "We have to look out for each other."

Nish just stood there blinking.

To Travis, it seemed the thought they could be teammates had never once crossed Nish's mind.

THE LIGHTS.

It was the brightness of the lights that astonished Travis more than anything else. It was as if the entire arena had been lit up by the sun itself. He had never seen such brilliant light in a hockey rink, never seen such sharp colours in the ice: pure white in the open areas; sea blue at the goalmouth; a rich, deep blue at centre ice, where the Toronto Maple Leafs logo was bigger than their entire dressing room back in Tamarack.

The Screech Owls were in the Air Canada Centre.

It had been the greatest experience so far of Travis Lindsay's young life. Mr. Dillinger had rented an old school bus for the team. Muck Munro had come along as coach – "But I'm not wearing any stupid *suit* behind the bench," he'd protested – and everyone's parents were coming down in car pools behind the players.

The three-hour drive south to Toronto had been a wild affair, with Nish threatening to moon the cars following behind – right up until Sarah advised him that his own mother was in the car directly behind the bus.

Data and Fahd had played their video games. Jenny had listened to her music downloads. Wilson had his mother's cellphone and used it to take pictures of the kids and send them back to his father, who had to work that day. Gordie and Derek fell asleep. Willie skimmed through a thick copy of *The Guinness Book of World Records*. Dmitri read a comic book.

And Nish was out of control.

He taught Simon how to make farting noises by cupping his open hand under his armpit and flapping his arm like a wing. He showed Liz how to crack her knuckles. He threw a hundred raspberries Sarah's direction, and she took a hundred good shots at him for being an idiot.

It was the strangest relationship Travis had ever seen. Sarah seemed to love poking at Nish, and Nish seemed to love striking back. It was like they were only *pretending* to be enemies so they could take shots at each other.

Travis still wasn't sure about his own relationship with the chubby little kid he'd first called the "Nincompoop." It had definitely changed since that first awful week.

But all that had faded. No one ever called Travis "Zipper Boy" anymore, or even mentioned the incident. The mysterious disappearance of Sidney the screech owl had never been solved, even though three of the kindergarten class knew exactly what had happened. Sarah had never said anything, and neither had Travis. They trusted that Nish had learned his lesson and would never do such a thing again.

What had changed things more than anything was the little hockey team and the invitation to come to Toronto and take part in the *Hockey Day in Canada* celebrations. The team had brought the kids together. They felt almost like brothers and sisters now, as if the team and their name, the Screech Owls, and their new jerseys made them all part of one little group that looked out for each other. Just as Sarah had said to Nish that morning when Sidney made his real break for freedom.

Nish was annoying, yes, but also entertaining – again, just as Sarah had said he would prove to be. He kept things going both in the class and on the team. When the kids weren't talking to him, they were talking about him. And Travis, much to his own surprise, no longer felt jealous because of it. Nish was just being Nish, which meant he would naturally be the centre of attention.

He had been the centre of attention on the way down, with his farting noises and belches and raspberries and silly yelling, and he had been the centre of attention at the Hockey Hall of Fame, which the little team had visited in the afternoon. It was Nish who'd taken the earphones in the Broadcast Zone and called a play-by-play almost as well as the announcers did on television. It was Nish who had taken the hardest shot in the little rink where they could measure shots. And it was Nish who, when the kids were staring in awe at the bronze plaques honouring all those great players who had been named to the Hall – Gretzky, Orr, Beliveau, Howe, Richard, Lafleur, Messier, Lemieux – had pounded his fist against a blank space on the wall.

"Here's where they'll put my face," he announced.

Sarah shook her head in disgust. "Your *butt* will make the Hall of Fame before your *face* ever will."

MR. DILLINGER WAS SETTING OUT THE NEW jerseys, checking numbers against a players list and carefully hanging each jersey above the head of the player who would be wearing it.

Travis reached high and took down his number 7. He pulled it slowly over his head, kissing the new crest as it passed by his face. The crest had come out fairly well. Liz's drawing did look like an owl, not a bear, as Nish had claimed, but the hockey puck looked more like a black hole the little bird was about to fall into.

If this group of kids stayed together, and if they kept calling themselves the Screech Owls, Travis said to himself, they'd one day have to get a professional logo – just like the pros had.

Sarah, sitting to one side of Travis, helped him work the back of the jersey over his shoulder pads. The kids had no parents to help them; Muck had insisted they do everything as a team, with no distractions.

Parents weren't allowed in the little dressing room that had been assigned to the Owls. Mr. Dillinger would tighten the skates of any kid who felt they couldn't do the job themselves.

When Muck came into the room, Travis saw he had dressed up for the occasion – at least "dressed up" as far as Muck Munro was concerned. He had on a track suit and a turtleneck. He was wearing new sneakers.

Muck also had a speech. It was seven words long.

"Let's go out and have some fun."

The Owls cheered and hammered their sticks on the floor, then bounced up and began filing out, Mr. Dillinger checking as they passed him at the doorway that each player had his or her neck guard on and helmet strap done up tightly.

Sarah tapped Travis on the shin pads as the little team made its way down the corridor over the rubber matting and out toward the entrance to the Air Canada Centre ice surface.

"Neat," Sarah said.

"Awesome."

Nish was just ahead of them, looking twice as wide, with his big hockey pants, as any of the other Owls.

As they came out into the rink, Travis thought the burst of light and sound – rock music blaring from the scoreboard – was like having his helmet rapped with a hockey stick. It stunned him.

Nish, on the other hand, was waving to the crowd as if he'd just been chosen first star of the NHL game after a shootout where he had been the only player able to score.

"I can't believe how many fans came out just to see *me*!" he shouted back to Sarah, who gave him a push in the back that sent him spilling out the gate and nose-first onto the ice, where he slid halfway to centre.

The Air Canada Centre erupted with laughter and cheers.

Nish surprised Travis. Instead of lying there and starting to bawl – as he would have done not so long before – Nish got up, pretended to dust himself off, and then bowed to the crowd in all four directions.

A huge cheer went up in response.

The Brantford 9.9s were already on the ice, spinning around in their own end. They looked bigger, older, stronger, faster, better. . . . Travis hoped the Owls wouldn't embarrass themselves. After all, the little team from Tamarack had never played an actual game before.

This wouldn't be a real game, either. They had only a few minutes to play before the Zambonis came out to clear the ice for the next period of the NHL game. The referee who would be handling their mini-game moved to get things going immediately by blowing his whistle and calling them to centre ice.

No time for a warm-up. No chance for Travis to try out his new idea of aiming to ring one off the crossbar for good luck.

Travis's line would be starting, with Nish and Fahd back on defence and Jeremy in goal.

Sarah lined up opposite a Brantford kid who seemed twice her size. The players opposite them looked more like peewees than beginners. Had there been a mistake? Travis wondered.

But it was too late for questions. The referee raised his hand and dropped the puck. And the Screech Owls' very first hockey game was on.

IT WAS INSTANTLY EMBARRASSING.

The big centre for Brantford clipped the puck away the moment the hard rubber disk struck the ice.

His winger, equally big, bowled over Dmitri as they raced for the puck, the bigger player scooping it up and firing a pass straight back to the big centre, who split the Owls defence of Nish and Fahd so fast it seemed they weren't even wearing skates.

He fired the puck right between Jeremy's legs, and Jeremy, spinning around to see where the puck had gone, lost his balance and fell over backwards.

The crowd roared with laughter.

Brantford 9.9s 1, Screech Owls 0. Less than five seconds into the game!

Everything was different. The crowd – probably as many as twelve thousand fans still sitting in their seats for the intermission – was roughly twelve thousand times larger than any crowd that had ever watched the Owls before. The noise from the scoreboard was deafening. The lights were blinding. The ice seemed *hot* rather than cold. Travis's legs felt like wet noodles.

The referee went immediately to another faceoff to hurry the little match along. This time, Sarah tried her trick of plucking the puck out of the air, and it worked. She fired the puck over to Travis, who sent it across to Dmitri.

Only to have the big centre intercept it!

He came flying up the ice again and tried the same play – only this time, instead of splitting the Tamarack defence, he ran straight into the wall.

The wall known as Wayne Nishikawa.

The Brantford player went down hard, spinning into the corner. Nish skated over fast, and he leaned over to help the big centre up, saying, "Sorry, sorry, sorry – I didn't mean to."

The referee was also there, and he took Nish at his word. "Don't worry kid, no one's hurt."

Nish turned and winked at Sarah and Travis. Sarah started giggling. "I *love* this idiot!" she said to Travis.

Muck called them off for the next shift, sending out Derek's line, and the Brantford team almost scored again, another big forward ringing a shot off the post behind Jeremy.

Time was quickly running out. Muck leaned over the heads of the three forwards and talked to them. "Nothing skates as fast as a puck," he said to them. "Let the puck work for you."

Next shift out, Sarah got the puck and sent a long pass up the side. Dmitri, skating faster than anyone else on the ice, the big Brantford centre included, caught up to it and swept it in on goal. His backhand shot was stopped by the little Brantford goaltender, who was practically lying down to cover the net, but the rebound came to Sarah, and she very calmly lifted the puck over the goalie and into the net.

Tie game.

Derek's line again held off the Brantford charge. Travis looked at the clock. He figured one last shift for his line and that would be it. The Zambonis would be out and the big NHL game would start up again.

They would only have one more chance.

This time, the puck went deep into the Owls' end, and Nish hurried back to get it. The big centre gave chase, however, and they reached the puck together, the centre crashing full speed into Nish from behind.

Nish went down, hard, and lay there.

Travis looked at the referee. The ref had instinctively raised his arm to call a penalty, but then remembered the game was purely for fun and almost over. Still, there was to be no body contact, and this had obviously been deliberate. Before he could blow the whistle, however, Nish was back up on his skates and had taken the puck away from the big centre.

Nish was moving down the ice with it now, carrying the puck out over the blue line.

Travis was racing to join the rush when suddenly he was aware of something very strange.

There was clapping in the stands. They were cheering on Nish, the little kid who'd taken a dive at the start of the game and who had just been hit by a dirty blow behind the net.

Nish was twisting and turning, somehow managing to hold onto the puck while the Brantford team tried to catch him. One player tried to trip Nish and he simply danced over the swinging stick, still in control of the puck.

Nish looked up, saw Travis, and fed him a perfect pass.

The puck seemed to weigh more than an elephant to Travis. His legs were like rubber. But he dug in and skated with the puck. Up over centre, past the Brantford winger opposite, who tried to poke check him and missed.

Sarah was calling for the puck, banging her stick on the ice.

Travis sent the puck on his backhand toward her, wishing instantly his stick blade didn't have such a big curve as the puck sort of sputtered off line. But Sarah was still able to catch it in her skates and kick it up onto her blade.

This time, Sarah tried to split the two Brantford defence. Seeing it coming, they decided to squeeze Sarah out of the play and take the puck from her when she couldn't go any further. But Sarah saw the move and dished off to the other side, where Dmitri was waiting for the puck.

Dmitri, using his speed, deked around the defence closest to him and swooped behind the net. He saw Travis coming in with no one around him, and fed the puck out to Travis.

Travis thought his heart was going to rip right through his throat guard. He knew he had the perfect shot. And he had his new composite stick with the curve in the blade.

Travis leaned into the shot as hard as he could.

The little Brantford goaltender went down to block it.

The puck seemed to move in slow motion. Travis saw it heading for a hole, and then saw the little goalie's blocker flash up to nick it as it was heading into the top of the net. The slight deflection was just enough to send the puck pinging off the crossbar. The very sound Travis had wanted to hear earlier now rang like an alarm.

He could hear the crowd groan in sympathy. But the referee still hadn't blown his whistle.

The puck popped up and rolled straight back, end-over-end, slapping on the ice near the top of the circle.

Nish was charging in at full speed toward it. And also coming in at full speed was the big centre that he'd hit and then later made a fool of.

It seemed Nish would win the race, until the big Brantford centre dove and took the legs out from under him. The Brantford player slid off toward the boards, but Nish, spinning like a top on the ice, was still headed toward the puck.

Travis had never imagined anything quite like what he saw next. He watched as Nish, sliding and spinning, somehow turned his head so he could see the puck. Nish twisted himself so his stick was flat on the ice. And when he spun one final time into the puck, he had his stick positioned so it caught the puck perfectly.

He used his arms to give the shot an extra lift – and then spun on, so he couldn't even see what happened next.

And what happened next was that the puck flew through the air like a golf chip, rolling up and over the players sprawled in front of the Brantford net and the little goaltender who had gone down to block Travis's shot.

And into the net.

Screech Owls 2, Brantford 9.9s 1.

Tamarack wins.

Buzzer and referee's whistle went at the same time.

The Owls poured through the bench gate, onto the ice, and straight for Nish, now lying flat on his back, his big red face gleaming under the television lights of the Air Canada Centre.

Travis and Sarah were the first ones there, and both threw themselves on top of Nish.

Travis looked into the stands. Thousands of fans were giving Nish a standing ovation.

It was unbelievably loud. But even in the uproar, Travis was still sure he could hear Nish saying something.

It sounded like "*Your star has arrived.*"

Where had he heard that before?

THE END